Quarter Rats

ALMOST A TRUE STORY

J. R. Klein

Publisher: Del Gato
Editor: Laura Rehfeld Davis
Library of Congress Control Number: 2021907450
ISBN: 978-1-7368101-0-1
ISBN: 978-1-7368101-1-8 (ebook)

For Jeanne

And for the many great Quarter Rats I have known

Also by J. R. Klein

Frankie Jones
The Ostermann House
To Find: The Search for Meaning in Life on The Gringo Trail
A Distant Past, An Uncertain Future
The Visitor
The Code
Times Like These
All the Burning Rooftops
If I Could Do It All Again
The Sacred and the Damned

1

I walk through the French Quarter. It is late. The night is hot and dark. The glitter and noise from the bars are gone. I avoid Bourbon Street—this time of night it smells of spilled beer dried onto the flagstone sidewalks. In the morning they will scrub it clean again. Tonight, I use Royal Street. Other nights I go down Dauphine. Both are less filled with tourists.

I've lived in the Quarter for a couple of years. I used to think it was a happy place. Then later, a melancholy place. Now, it's just a place where I live and spend all my time. I don't know why I think about this junk late at night walking down Royal Street after work. Well, one thing I can tell you is that I am a very philosophical person. A lot of times I wonder why we think the same dumb thoughts over and over. There must be a reason…probably. I already pretty much have the answer to that.

I glance up at a balcony as I pass. A light is on. I see the glow of a lamp as it spreads through the lace curtains of the French doors of Ramona's place. I wonder if she is alone. I wonder but keep going.

I am a Quarter Rat. For no special reason I think about that for a second; it makes me feel neither happy nor sad. Yes, I am a Quarter Rat, those of us who live here, who live off the tourists. Well, I do, in any event. How long do you have to live in the French Quarter to be a Quarter Rat? I wonder about this as I look at the blue-gray flagstone beneath my feet. How long? For a while probably, but not long. Long enough to know which cafés are good cafés, the ones that Quarter Rats trust, which parts of the city belong to the tourists, which to the Rats.

My name is Rubin—Rubin Kranovich. I came to New Orleans from Baltimore. If you were to ask why, I couldn't quite tell you. Does it matter—those decisions we make that are unclear when we make them and are even less clear now?

On down Royal Street I go. A musician packs up. Straps her collapsible stool onto a motorbike. Sets her violin in a case and buckles it shut. She doesn't look over at me as I pass—one less face to see, one less smile to smile back at I suppose. Barely ten steps farther on I hear the putter of the motorbike as it speeds off anxious to be gone, leaving behind the vapor of its exhaust.

The sky holds a shade of vermilion. There's a color for you…vermilion. I heard someone use it once to describe the sky and now I use it all the time. Of course, it could just be the reflection of something red. A rooftop, for example. Red sky at night sailor's delight. I think about that. They used to say that when I lived in Baltimore. They have lots of sailors there. My grandfather was one back in Russia. He was a fisherman. That's why he ended up in Baltimore…to be near the water.

I stick my hands in my pockets. I could walk over to Bourbon Street where the bars are open all night and have a drink. Most of the tourists will be gone at this hour. A few Rats like me will be inside clinging to a drink. It's a thought, but nothing more. Anyhow, I could just as easily have stopped at The Chart Room. My eye caught a glimpse of it as I crossed Bienville and looked over to Chartres Street, but I kept walking.

I pass Saint Anne Street where Sebastian lives. He's probably my closest friend. Everyone calls him Sab. I continue on until I reach Ursilines and then turn left and cut over to Burgundy and then go two blocks more. The red sky is fading. It now holds a pale purple-blackish color with some stars spread across it.

I enter the courtyard where there are two sets of apartments, one to my left and one to my right joined by another set straight ahead. They go by the name of slave quarters. That's what they're called if you want to rent one. They're the places where a long time ago the slaves once lived. They took care of the white folks in the Quarter. And of course, being slaves they didn't get crap for doing it. Just a shitty little room to live in. Now, they're cheap apartments for people like me—the Rats. I pass Virginia who is coming down the stairs. She smiles a little and goes on. She's always in and out at odd hours.

When I walk through the courtyard at night I think for a second about the people who lived in these tiny apartments a long time ago. I imagine they're still here, the slaves, up in the apartments in the heat of the night lying on skinny, thin cots made of wooden planks and straw. I pretend I'm one of those people stuck in a trap that I can't get out of. Looking at the bare ceiling from my cot. I wonder why we imagine a world that is worse than the one we live in now? Oh, well.

2

In the morning I'm up feeling good. I slept well. The purring of the window AC kept the heat away. I'm stiff but I tell myself I am too young to be stiff. Old people have those problems; I am not old yet. I feel like I will never be old. I see old people walking through the Quarter hopping along, hunched, legs like twigs. I don't think I'll ever be like that.

I pull myself off the bed and stand up straight as one of those Continental Soldier guys we used to hear about when we were kids. I look at myself in the bedroom mirror. I look fine. I take a shower and get dressed—jeans and T-shirt—and leave the apartment. I am a slave, laughing to no one but myself. I walk down the stairs holding the warm wrought iron railing. Of course, I don't need to hold the railing, but I do anyway.

Down Burgundy Street I go until I get to Toulouse and there I enter a café. I wonder if Ramona will be there. A nod to Franka, the waitress. She smiles. I go through the café to the outdoor courtyard. A whole bunch of small birds dart around in the vines above me. I sit at a table. Franka comes out with coffee. She's always very quick when she serves you. She will bring my quiche in a second, she tells me.

I want to light a cigarette but I don't have one and anyway I quit and haven't smoked in months. Not that I really needed to quit. Heck, I could probably run a marathon and not even break a sweat.

I stretch my arms and for no special reason I find myself thinking about my job. Did I tell you I work at a hotel on Canal Street? It's a real fancy, real hoity-toity. I'm the doorman, the bellhop you might say. I wear a red jacket and a white shirt and one of those red caps like organ grinder monkeys wear. It makes me look like a real jerk, but in all honesty I don't mind so much. The hotel pays very little but I rake it in on tips. I usually work from four in the afternoon until midnight. On a good day I can make two hundred bucks, sometimes more. You wouldn't believe how many people will slip you a sawbuck for opening the door or schlepping a bag ten feet or helping them get a cab. It has something to do with people being on vacation or whatever. They think they have tons of money to burn.

Well, all in all I make out pretty good if you consider I only report a little of what I make on my taxes. No one knows how much money I make, least of all Uncle Sam. The hotel says they know and that I should report it all, but I know it's a lot of BS.

So, at the end of the year when I do my taxes I water it way down to make it look like I make almost nothing. And anyway, if one of those G-men guys from the IRS came by and saw the crappy place I live in he'd probably turn around and leave pretty quick.

Does it bother me, then, that I'm bilking the government like this? Well, think of it this way—how many of the real fat-cats, the millionaires and billionaires let's say, how many of them report every ducat they make? Not very many, you can be sure of that. I'm talking about folks who have *real* money. Like the guy who slipped me a C-note for toting his bag ten feet. He stuck it in my hand and squeezed my hand shut so I wouldn't drop it. He probably felt sorry for me for having to dress up like a capuchin monkey. Probably is what happened.

You can tell the people who feel that way when they see me. They look and scrunch their nose and blink a couple of times. A friend of mine, a real smart guy, told me that blinking like that is one of those brainstem responses that people do without thinking. I'm not sure where our brainstem is but I believe him anyway.

Clifford Ritter walks into the café and comes over and sits at my table. We used to be real good friends—well, we still are, actually. He doesn't say anything for a while. He just rubs his forehead and sits quietly. That's how Clifford is when he joins me in the café. He says nothing for a while. I'm pretty sure he's thinking about what he wants to say. He's a very precise person, that's what I've noticed.

"Another hot day," he finally says, looking up at the big thick branches above us. He pretends to wipe beads of sweat from his forehead though he's not sweating—something to embellish his comment no doubt. He's good at that, at adding a gesture here and there. Lots of times I tell him he should be an actor. He just laughs and never takes me seriously. It seems we don't pay attention much to what other people tell us to do.

"Wanna hear something crazy?" he says.

This is another thing he does. He describes everything as crazy. It's one of his favorite phrases even though he rarely tells you anything crazy.

"The thermometer outside my window said it was eighty-nine degrees."

Hardly crazy, I think. Not at this time of year at least.

"And that was pretty early this morning."

I nod and shrug.

"No, that's what it said."

I nod again so he doesn't have to repeat it. He can get annoying as shit, saying everything two and three times or so.

Clifford has been a Quarter Rat longer than I have. He was here when I arrived. Came from somewhere out west, maybe California...I don't remember where.

He's a cabbie—a hack, we called them in Baltimore. He works the afternoons and late into the evening. No one knows his way around N.O. better than Clifford. He knows every street, every corner, every neighborhood—the good ones and the bad ones. There are plenty of them he never goes into. It's hard enough dealing with drunks and tourists who aren't sure where they want to go. It's a whole different matter when you get a pack of teenagers who want you to take them on a joyride to some netherworld and then when you get there they leap out of the cab and tear off in all different directions without paying you. It happened to Clifford once, but he tells the story a lot.

"And it was hotter than hell's shingles last night, too," Clifford says, as if I didn't know it. "People complained about it all night long. Of course, it makes for good business. No one wants to walk in the heat. So I end up getting lots of little fares. Two blocks here, five blocks there. No one want to walk in all the heat. And they dump a big tip on you even though you just took them around the corner. Crazy, huh?"

There, see what I mean about crazy?

"Yeah…a big tip for going nowhere. Don't ask me why." He stops. He seems to be thinking about what he just said. His brow curls down for a second. But he seems to abandon the thought pretty quick. He says, "So anyway, about the heat. It's all due to global warming. I'm convinced of it. I've been here in the Quarter now for…let's see…for a long time. This is the hottest summer ever."

I don't think he actually did a study of it, but he's probably right.

"Saw Ramona this morning," Clifford says.

He knows Ramona and I sorta had a thing going. Not that it's over or anything. We still see each other quite a bit.

"She was over there on Royal Street."

He points in the wrong direction—totally wrong. I mean like a hundred and eighty degrees off. It bugs the shit out of me when people can't get their directions right. I always wonder how Clifford can be a hack and not know north from east.

Me, I have a great sense of direction. I remember reading that people like me have little bits of iron in their brain...particles or whatever. More than most people have. It's sort of like having a built-in compass. You probably don't believe me, but I read it in a good newspaper...like in the *Enquirer* I think it was.

Franka brings my quiche. Clifford gets a latte and an order of beignets. Quarter Rats never go to the *Café du Monde* for beignets. The Café du Maul, I call it. Filled with tourists in pink or green Bermuda shorts and T-shirts with pictures of things like the Eiffel Tower on them always kind of tipping over sideways. Don't get it. Anyway, I think they're trying to let you know all the places they've been.

I get a second cup of coffee. The quiche at this place is the best in all N.O. You might think making a quiche is easy but there's a real art to it. Most have soggy crusts. Those are the ones I hate most. I mean how hard can it be to get a stupid crust right?

"Going over to the West Bank today," Clifford says. "Taking the ferry." His lips and a spot on his nose have powdered sugar on them from the beignet. He'll be like that for the next ten minutes. I think it's why he's a hack. Nobody gives a shit what a hack looks like. All they care about is whether he can get them where they want to go and keep it cheap—not drive you halfway to hell and back. One thing about Clifford, he won't rob you. He could if he wanted to because most people don't know squat about how to get where they're going in N.O.

And I can tell you, there are lots of hacks in this city who will rob you blind. Squeeze ten bucks out of you for going a couple of blocks. It's easy to do according to Clifford, what with all the one-way streets and the weird names and all. Like Dauphine Street, for example. You hear every imaginable version of it from the conventioneers and tourists. I get it all the time at the hotel. Just the other day, this woman wants to know where Daffey Street is. It took plenty of thinking on my part to figure out what she meant. So then she points to it on a little map she has in her purse. There it is. Dauphine Street in plain English. How she got Daffey Street out of it I have no idea. I pulled out a fresh map and traced a route for her with a yellow highlighter I carry. I probably use that highlighter a hundred times a day. And are you ready for this? She drops a buck on me for drawing a line on a stupid map.

But of all the streets in the Quarter, Tchoupitoulas is the one they get wrong the most. I've heard every version of it, so I'm ready when they spring a new one on me. Sometimes I think they do it on purpose, just to see what I'll do. You know, watch the monkey get all confused.

The version I hear the most comes out something like Toolachoopas Street. "Excuse me young man, can you tell me where Toolachoopas Street is?"

I'm not gonna ask Clifford why he's going to the West Bank. You wouldn't do that unless you want to hear about everything he's been up to for the last month. See, he never gets straight to the point. It's like he gives you a historical perspective about it all. You know, like reading one of those ginormous Russian novels by Tolstoy or Dostoyevsky or Solzhenitsyn where they give you every stinking tidbit of info before they drop the real junk on you. Remember those books?

They took me an eternity to read in high school and most of them I never really finished. The Russian novelists could get away with doing that when you consider how they looked. They always had that big story look about them. Like remember how that Solzhenitsyn guy looked? You have to look like that if you're gonna write books that people are gonna be reading forever. That's what I think. Yeah, but Clifford has to give you every dopey detail before he gets to the point. And he doesn't look like a Russian novelist, not by a long shot, and he doesn't dress like one either. Imagine one of those guys wearing a Grateful Dead T-shirt...you know, like the one with the skeleton head on it and all?

And sure enough, Clifford doesn't really tell me why he's going to the West Bank, not right away, anyway. Instead, he starts by saying there's a shop over in Algiers that has a great selection of records. Vinyl. Thousands of them. Like maybe a million. He describes his collection of vinyl. And I have to admit, it does sound big. It's probably why he wears a Grateful Dead T-shirt a lot. His collection of Grateful Dead vinyl is huge...humongous is what I think he said.

But none of this has anything to do with why he's going to the West Bank. You'd think it does, wouldn't you? But it doesn't.

Well, all in all, I'm a pretty good listener. You have to be to do what I do at the hotel. Do you know how many times a day total strangers start telling me the story of their life? It usually begins with them explaining why they're in N.O. But they can't stop there. Oh no. They have to tell you where they're from and why they're here and how many kids they have and all their names. And me, I have to nod and smile. Don't forget, they'll be back in a while with their bags that they'll want me to dump into the back of some hack. You can see how well I got the pieces of this puzzle put together.

3

Later in the morning, I walk to the top of the Quarter to a shoe repair store, a cobbler's shop. Now that's a word you don't hear anymore…cobbler. But here in the Quarter, this guy still uses it. And he wears a leather apron, too. Probably wants to make his store seem quaint or old-fashioned. Well, it works.

And there's even a neon sign of a shoe that flashes on and off in the window. One of those high-topped shoes like they wore at the turn of the century. Why do we think stuff was so cool at the turn of the century? In fact, it all seems like it was pretty damn stupid to me.

At the turn of the century the French Quarter wasn't all that different from now, of course. No electricity, that's true. And no Quarter Rats greasin' on the tourists all the time. But the buildings and all were pretty much the same. Heck, some of the bars have been around for an eternity. Like Lafitte's Blacksmith shop and The Old Absinthe House, for example, over there on Rue Bourbon as it was known then. The places where Jean Lafitte and Andrew Jackson used to poke around in. I go there now and then when I'm sure it's mostly empty.

People get real tanked up drinking absinthe at the Absinthe House. That's what Clifford said. He picks up lots of people in his cab out front of the place.

So anyway, the cobbler shop is just a couple blocks back behind Bourbon Street in an area we call the back-of-the-quarter. I think I forgot to tell you that. It's called that because tourists don't go there much. Just a lot of little houses for Quarter Rats like me. Every now and then someone, a tourist, gets lost and ends up back there. You can recognize them instantly. They stare and look around real confused. No iron particles in the brain like I talked about. They usually stand and look around trying to get a fix on where they are or stare at a map they pulled from their pocket.

A couple of times when I was walking through the area one of them stopped me and said, "Excuse me Sonny, can you tell me where we are?" Oh, that's another thing, they love to call you Sonny when they don't know your name. They think they're being nice to you.

I should wear one of those paper stick-on badges the conventioneers use, the ones that say, Hello, My Name Is— The ones that you write in your name. I can fill it in so it says: Hello, My Name Is Sonny. That way when I walk through the Quarter they won't have to make up a name for me. Of course, some joker will probably say, "Hey, *look*, Martha, his name really *is* Sonny!"

Bad idea.

I'm gonna get new soles put on a pair of shoes. I like the

shoes, they are real comfortable. I wear them at the hotel. When you're on your feet for eight straight hours you need good leather...no roadkill. I could go get a pair of shoes at Payless; there's a store nearby over on Canal Street. It's always an option. But do you know how long those suckers last? And secondly, your feet are in total misery the whole time. The leather is like cardboard. Lots of people go to Payless to get a pair of shoes real cheap. They waste ten bucks on a tip and then buy a pair of crappy cardboard shoes. Figure that out.

I keep pretty far away from the heart of the Quarter—like Jackson Square is what I mean. The jugglers and mimes and painters and all that junk. I can't believe people still watch them, the mimes. I'm sure you know what I'm talking about. The ones who pretend they're caught in a glass box and can't get out. It's all stupid as shit. One time, though, I watched this guy for about two hours. I wanted to see how he was gonna quit when it was time for lunch or whatever. So sure enough, here's what he does. He pretends like he found a little door and opens it and steps out of the invisible box. Well, you can bet I felt pretty ripped off. And I actually gave the guy a quarter because I watched him for so long. Cripes, I wanted to go pull the quarter out of the black top hat he kept next to the invisible box...but I didn't.

I'm glad I'm not in the top hat business. Can you imagine, the only people buying them these days are street mimes? You've really gotta know what you're getting into before you start a business.

So I circle around to make sure I don't end up on the

wrong side of the Quarter while I'm heading to the cobbler. I like that word…cobbler. Anyway, with my sense of direction I don't worry much about making a wrong turn and find myself surrounded by a bunch of mimes and artists and a pack of marauding tourists—the ones who just came out of the *Café du Monde*. Geez, they're almost as bad as the drunks in the evening except this bunch is buzzing from all the caffeine. Funny, isn't it, they're both sort of out of control. And they both do real dumb stuff—like they buy paintings of clowns and crap like that. You waste all this money buying a painting of a clown and then what? Now you tell me, where the hell do you hang a painting of a clown in your house? I certainly wouldn't want one in my apartment. Like everything is going to be okay if you hang a picture of a clown on the wall…right? You know: *Don't Worry, Be Happy*. That was a song by Bobby McFerrin if I have it correct.

I walk into the cobbler shop. It's owned by a German guy—at least as far as I can tell from his accent, anyway. He might be faking it, you know, to make it sound like he's from the old world or something like that. But I think he really is from one of those old world places somewhere.

He looks at the shoes and says, "Ouh, yah, zees tings need some new letter, fer shur. Der pretty good shooz, tho. I can fix dem while ya wait…if ya want."

"Shuur," I say. Suddenly I'm talking like he is.

He goes in the back room. I hear him doing some tapping and then I hear something like a sewing machine.

I look around the shop. He has a bunch of shoes with

white tags on them that look like they're waiting to be picked up. In almost no time at all, he's back out with the shoes.

"Zer ya go. Zey should be fine now."

I look at them. "Wow, zees is fine," I say. I pay him and leave and head across the Quarter over to Sab's place on St. Anne Street. Last time I saw him he said he had something for me. He didn't say what but I think I know what it is. I make it pretty quickly over to Royal Street carrying my shoes. As I'm heading down Royal I run smack into Ramona, nearly colliding head-on coming around the corner.

She looks at me and smiles. Boy, am I happy to see her. And let me tell you, Ramona is beautiful. She has this dark black hair and these blue eyes…the bluest eyes you've ever seen. You almost never see that together—black hair and blue eyes.

I always thought the name Ramona was sort of odd, but I never said anything to her about it, especially when you consider we don't have a whole lot to say about the name we get. For example, when I was a kid there was this girl in school named Mesa Luna. It has something to do with the moon…that much I know. Well, let me tell you, Mesa Luna had to put up with lots of crap because of that name. They called her everything under the sun. Stuff like Looney Mesa, and Messy Luna. You can see how easy it would be to screw up a name like Mesa Luna. You can come up with a whole raft of shit. Even stuff like Mona Lisa. Oh yeah, and there was this guy I grew up with—we were actually pretty good friends in fact. His name was Justin and his last name was Case…Justin

Case. It's true, I swear.

Anyway, I felt Ramona's name was really quite pretty though I never told her so. I probably should, but I haven't.

Ramona works as a waitress at a joint on Bourbon Street. Another one of those jobs where you can really rake in the money. The tourists in N.O. throw money around like the damn sky is falling. It's worse than in Vegas. In Vegas you at least have a chance to get some of it back. Here, it's gone forever once you drop a tip on someone.

Ramona makes enough money to rent a pretty nice second-story place on Royal Street, one with a balcony and all. You can sit up there and see all the people going by carrying all the crap they bought in Jackson Square or in some ratty flea market in the Quarter. And they're always carrying a monstrous drink of some kind, probably a hurricane or something. And they all look out of breath and sweaty even when it's only ten o'clock in the morning. All the coffee and beignets at *Café du Monde* don't help any.

I always worry one of them is going to go belly-up on the sidewalk below us and I'm going to have to rush down and do the CPR thing. I know how to do it. They wanted me to learn for my job at the hotel in case someone goes flat as a carp in front of me.

Ramona invites me up to her place. You get there from a little alley that you have to kind of sneak through to get to a set of stairs in the back that goes to the second floor.

When we get inside, the place is real comfy…the window AC is on and it's a pretty good one. Not like mine which you think is gonna gork out on you at any second. Her place always smells real nice, too. Sorta like mangos or whatever.

Ramona sets a bag on the chair. She's been out shopping. I don't know for what. She shops a lot…and buys some pretty nice stuff. She has great taste, not like me. I don't know how it is some people have great taste when it comes to clothes. Like everything seems to match and look good is what I mean. I can't do it. But then, mostly I just wear jeans and a T-shirt. So how hard can it be to get that right?

But Ramona, she dresses nice all the time. Lots of times she wears these real skimpy shorts and a tank top of some kind. I'm pretty certain that's what they're called…tank tops, from what little I know about women's clothes. She has a bunch of them that have thin little straps, spaghetti straps is what I think they're called. Wow, she looks great!

Well, it's way too hot to sit out on her balcony and watch the people below, that's for sure, so we sit in the living room. It's a real nice place, the living room. It has two sets of French doors that go out to the balcony. Both have these real nice lace curtains over them—Belgian lace probably. Isn't that what it is? I think I mentioned it when I walked past Ramona's place last night. Remember?

The lace goes real well with the doors. For one thing it's pretty as hell. If Belgians do one thing well, you'd have to say it's making great lace. But I think they also make good chocolate. Real rich stuff. Much better than Hershey's. Someone gave me a box of Belgian chocolate once as a tip at the hotel. At first I thought it was a pretty crappy tip and got sorta pissed until I got home and had a piece. Wow, you wouldn't believe that stuff! It might have been some Belgian folks who gave it to me. I have no way of knowing. Everyone looks pretty much the same in Bermuda shorts and T-shirts and flip-flops and with a big Panama hat on, even if you're from Belgium and not from Panama. You see lots of guys in the Quarter wearing them—Panama hats.

"I bought some real neat things," Ramona tells me. She's sitting across from me in a chair with a bag next to her. "Here, let me show you."

She gets up and takes off her jeans. She's standing there in a pair of real teeny panties. Yikes! I mean these things are practically transparent. She takes out a pair of shorts from the bag and holds them in front of her for a second and then gets into them and zips them up. You would think they were custom made by a tailor, that's how well they fit.

"What do you think?" she says. She turns around and then to the side. "You wouldn't know it but these were on sale."

She tells me what she paid. It doesn't mean much to me, not knowing the price of women's clothes and all. But they probably were a bargain even considering the skimpy little bit of cloth it took to make them.

She pulls another pair from the bag, takes off the first, and puts the second one on. These are real different from the first. They're seersucker things, blue and white striped things. And are they ever short! Yikes! She models these as well. Kinda like those women who are on the runway. You know what I mean, the ones who show off the new styles in New York or Paris or someplace. Well, that's what Ramona does. She walks across the room, turns in a real snappy way, and walks back.

It's no wonder she rakes it in when she's slinging drinks on Bourbon Street. She's allowed to wear anything she wants—not like me. All she has to do is tie a little four-inch apron around the front for her money and tips and all. But even that makes her look terrific at work.

So, she has two pairs of shorts and a new tank top. A lavender thing. I have to confess, lavender is not my favorite color but it's perfect for Ramona. You can picture it: her with her olive-colored skin and black hair and a lavender tank top. Sure enough, she takes off the tank top she's wearing and puts on the new one. *Aye, yi, yi!*

She holds her hands out as if to say, what'dya think?

Well I'm thinking a lot, you can be sure of that. I mean, here we are in her living room that's all cooled down by the AC and the place smells like mangos and here's Ramona in her new shorts with her brand-new lavender tank top on. I'm sure you get the picture.

Okay, you might be wondering by now where all this is going, right? All this stuff I've been telling you about me and the Quarter and all is what I mean. But you see, that's the thing about the Quarter, you have no idea what's gonna happen next. It's perfect for me, being a real spontaneous sort of guy. I mean look what happened here. I was heading over to Sab's and here I am watching a fashion show by Ramona instead. And I still might go over to Sab's. It depends on what Ramona has in store.

My instincts tell me she has something planned for us today. They say humans don't have instincts but I can tell you they do.

Ramona's still wearing her new shorts and the new tank top. She goes over to one of the French doors and looks out for a second, then gets a glass of lemonade, one for each of us, and sits next to me.

4

One thing I didn't tell you is I'm a pretty good-looking guy. That's what I've been told though I don't believe it. I guess you could say I have real low self-esteem. Otherwise, how could I do what I do at the hotel? How many people would want a job where you dress up like a monkey?

I spend most of the day at Ramona's until she has to go to work at three o'clock. She takes a shower and comes out smelling like lilacs or like one of those real sweet flowers that grow all over the French Quarter. Whatever it is, it's great.

And then to top things off, she's wearing one of her new pairs of shorts and the lavender tank top to work. Geez Louise, this is someone who knows how to dress. You know she'll be back tonight with a wad of bills big enough to choke old *T. rex.*

I never actually make it to Sab's. Maybe tomorrow. I end up back at my place. Boy, it's hot out, let me tell you. You walk two blocks in this and water pours off you. You have to drink tons of fluid when it's like this or you shrivel up to nothing. And I mean nothing.

The temp in my apartment is pretty good. Not quite as nice as Ramona's, but not all that bad so long as I don't start doing jumping jacks or something stupid like that.

I don't have to work today…it's my day off. I think I forgot to tell you that. It's why I ran the errand, going to the cobbler is what I mean. I also forgot to tell you I left my shoes at Ramona's, the ones from the cobbler. You can see right away what part of the problem is. I can't remember crap. Basically, it's usually because I'm not paying attention too much. I'm not all that stupid and I'm not old and sure as hell I'm not senile.

But just out of curiosity I do a couple of jumping jacks. I'm wondering if I am senile or even sort of old. Well, I'm not, because I can jump like crazy. You should see me. Needless to say I only do a couple because the sweat is already collecting on my forehead. Cripes, if people could see what we do when no one's watching.

Apartments like mine are tiny places. They have three rooms—a miniscule bedroom, a bathroom, and a living room, if you want to call it that. And it has one of those pullman kitchens, I think that's what they're called, sorta stuck in the corner of the living room. It has a couple of windows that face out onto the second floor walkway that has a nice wrought iron railing like you see all over N.O.

I'm glad I don't work today because Ramona wore me out. One thing about Ramona…she has *lots* of energy.

I crash for a couple of hours. It's already around four o'clock when I wake up. Boy, am I hungry!

Fortunately, there's a place down on the corner. It's called Buster's. It has a couple of tables and a few chairs but it's mostly take-out stuff. This place has the best PoBoys in all of N.O. Not that I've tried them all, but I bet it does. And probably the best gumbo, too.

You can go to K-Paul's, the place in the middle of the Quarter, and get some great gumbo, but it's a real touristy joint. Tons of people line up outside everyday like a bunch of starving grasshoppers. Even so, Paul Prudhomme was a master at cooking.

But Buster's is just as good and barely a hundred yards from my place and no lines of people waiting to get in. And it's real cheap. Always just a few Quarter Rats inside, but that's about all.

So I get a sausage PoBoy, my absolute fav. And a big bottle of Mr. Pibb. I never heard of Mr. Pibb before I came to N.O., mostly because it's a southern kind of drink, far as I know. That's what I'm guessing, anyway. I eat my PoBoy. I pile lots of extra remoulade sauce on it. It really gooses up the flavor.

I've got a pretty good idea I'm going over to The Chart Room later. It's about the only bar I ever go to. It's over on the corner of Chartres and Bienville. The place is stuffed with Quarter Rats. Infested! But that's what I like.

They have big, tall windows, French doors actually, that are always open to the sidewalk and inside it's sort of dark and real mysterious, you could say. It used to be smoky as hell inside but now you have to go outside to smoke.

When you're sitting inside you get this great view of all the tourists walking up and down the Quarter, which is actually about as close as I want to get to them. Sometimes they stop and crank their neck in the open windows and gawk for a second. Of course, they never come in. They can tell right away it's not a tourist joint.

Every now and then someone famous walks past. Like I was sitting at a table next to the window one time with Sab and you're not gonna believe who walks by. Jim Nabors! Remember him? He did the Gomer Pyle guy on TV. He was tall and skinny and weird looking…and a Marine, a U.S. Marine, if you can imagine that. I could never understand how they expected us to believe someone like him could get into the Marines. Seriously?

Anyhow, Jim Nabors comes along and someone in The Chart Room recognizes him and says, "Hey, Jim, is that you?"

Sure enough, he stops and sticks out his hand to shake. Movie stars do that, I've noticed, they'll shake anyone's hand.

So they ask him why he's in N.O. and he says he's visiting friends. Says he came from Hawaii where he grows macadamia nuts. I heard macadamia nuts are real expensive, but have you ever heard of anyone actually eating a macadamia nut?

The other thing about Jim Nabors is he has this great voice. He talks with a kind of high squeaky voice and then when he starts singing it gets deep as hell. I don't get it. And he likes to sing songs like that one…you know, the one with the words *To Dream the Impossible Dream*. Junk like that.

And wouldn't you know it, right away someone says,

"Hey, Jim, sing a song. Come on. Sing a song."

Like the guy's gonna start singing right there on the Bienville Street outside The Chart Room.

He smiles with that big grin of his but he doesn't sing. He seems like a nice fella, all in all. I didn't want to bug him. I bet he gets bugged a lot so I just asked him for his autograph.

That's what it's like sitting near a window in The Chart Room. The French Quarter moves past you and you sit still. It's a lot like being on that moving thing at the airport to get to the next terminal where you stand there and everyone moves past you in the other direction. It's kind of like that.

5

It turns out I do end up in The Chart Room. As soon as I walk in, I stop and look around to see who's there. I don't see anyone I know right off, which is good because there are quite a few people I'd rather not get stuck talking to. Like Horace Slagg, for example. He can be real annoying. He's a photographer. That's what Sab told me. He's known Horace for years. Horace likes to hang around Sab, partly because they're photographers, but the real reason is because Sab always has tons of women around him. You see, Sab's real cool looking and has blond hair and a blond beard. And boy does he know how to turn on the love light.

You might think all Quarter Rats are young but that's not true. They come in all ages and sizes and shapes. I'm not sure how old Horace is—maybe fifty, who knows. He's originally from New York; you can tell when he talks. I could imitate it, but I'd rather not.

Anyway, it turns out Horace is a real famous photographer, that's what Sab says. And I'm sure Horace will tell you if you are dumb enough to get anywhere near him and get screwed to having to listen to him. When he starts talking you can't stop him. It comes out in one mammoth run-on sentence. I guess he thinks that when he tells the chicks hanging around Sab about all the stuff he's done they'll fall in love with him or something ridiculous like that. *News Flash: ain't gonna happen, Horace.*

He's told me the story of his photography stuff so many times I can repeat it like it's a multiplication table from the third grade. I'll just give you the CliffsNotes version.

First, he worked for *Time Magazine* way back when. I was in Horace's studio with Sab once. The walls were covered with pictures he took that were on the cover of *Time Magazine*. Yikes, you should see it!

Then he got tired of that and went to Paris and did fashion photography for Christian Dior.

And then, last, he did underwater photography with Jacques Cousteau. No, I'm serious. The deal is that Horace grew up in Miami and learned to dive when he was a kid. Hard to believe this guy could actually be a good scuba diver. But he is...if you believe Horace. And he does have lots of pictures of himself with Jacques Cousteau on his walls.

Just the same, he's one annoying SOB.

Well, no Horace tonight...not yet. But I'm probably safe even if he does come in because he never talks to me, just Sab. Like why would he talk to a dweeb like me, right? Makes you wonder why he even bothers coming to The Chart Room given that it's mostly full of dweebs and Rats and other dopes. Now there's a real fifty cent word for you—dweeb. I heard someone use it once and later looked it up and now I use it all the time. I like to use words like that. It makes me seem like I'm a hell of a smart guy…I think.

I sit at the bar and order a beer. They have scads of imported beers but the joint is really just a Local Joe sort of place, so I order a Bud.

Sometimes when there are lots of Rats in the place everybody starts doing tequila shooters. Fortunately, I don't have to drive so I don't worry about running over some stupid tourist or slamming my car into a gas lamp and causing an explosion or junk like that. And anyway, I don't have a car.

But the worst thing we do at The Chart Room is drink Irish Coffee. It was a big craze for a while. I actually think Sab or Horace was the perp who got everyone going on it.

Irish Coffee will blow you straight into the stratosphere. It's much worse than tequila…a gazillion times worse. You see, you have this drink that is nothing but coffee and a shot or two of Irish whiskey. And sometimes they slap a glob of whipped cream on top to make it look fancy. Well, the coffee blasts you off and the whiskey sends you into a nosedive. It short circuits your whole body.

It's even worse than the Boilermakers we used to drink back in Baltimore. We'd go to the corner bars in Highlandtown where I grew up. A Boilermaker is a pint of beer and a shot of whiskey. But the deal is, you dump the whiskey *into* the beer—it gooses the alcohol content of the beer way up. And I mean *way* up. A couple of Boilermakers and you're gone. Of course, in Highlandtown you only have to walk about a block or two to get home. Sort of like here in the Quarter.

These things, the Boilermakers, have all kinds of different names depending upon where you're from. A buddy of mine told me that. He's a bartender in Highlandtown. You have to know all the names in case someone comes in and rattles one off and you don't know what he's talking about. You have to be real sharp to be a bartender…*real* sharp. So, these Boilermakers, sometimes they're called a Citywide Special, or a Two-Step, or a Git-Right. Probably, there are even more names. As for me, I still like the old name Boilermaker.

So, I'm sucking on my Bud when this guy Eddie Clabberman comes in and sits on a stool next to me. I've known Eddie for quite a while. Eddie and Horace are like day and night.

Eddie's sort of quiet and he never brags, mostly because he has almost nothing to brag about…well, not yet. I'm figuring he'll be a real famous writer someday. That's what I'm figuring. I mean, the guy writes all the time. He writes so much you'd think he'd have finished ten books by now.

Of course, it takes a long time to write a book. That's what he always tells me. I get a little worried thinking he'll never finish this book of his.

He always tells me it's really huge—a tome is what he said. That's another one of those fifty-cent words. I had to look it up. Eddie's tome has something to do with a Quarter Rat who's always ripping people off…mostly even other Rats. Those are the worst kind of Rats. That's about all Eddie's said about his tome, which makes me think he hasn't gotten very far toming yet.

Eddie has worked all over the Quarter. His last job, well second to last job, was at *Café du Monde*. For a little while anyway. Said it practically drove him crazy and that he might need to start seeing a shrink. Of course he never did, being how much it costs for just one visit to one of those guys. And anyway, you don't get cured all that much from just one visit.

I heard it may take lots of time before these guys, the shrinks, can get stuff working again. And even then there's no guarantee you won't flip right back. It happens all the time. People do great and then, wham, they're right back where they were a few weeks ago—doing all the weird crap they were doing before. I'm glad I don't have to worry about that, at least not too much.

Well, Eddie all but flipped out just working at *Café du Monde*. So now he rides around the Quarter on one of those horse buggies. You see them all over. The ones where tourists are crammed into the back and the driver tells them about all the crap he thinks they want to know when they ride past some famous place. But it's easy to make stuff up, too. You just say something like, "And over here on the right is the house that Truman Capote lived in." And the people in the back of the buggy squeeze over and lean out to see the house.

Sometimes I have to wave down one of these buggy drivers when I'm working at the hotel. Then, a whole gob of tourists climb on the buggy. I always feel sorry for the horse, having to drag them all over the Quarter and getting nothing but a bag of oats.

Eddie orders a Bud also. Actually, a Bud and an ice-cold glass. Always an ice-cold glass.

"How's the tome?" I ask Eddie. I call it that these days, the tome, since I don't know anything else about the book.

Eddie smiles a little but not very much. Actually, I'm real good at body language, but Eddie's sorta hard to figure out because he always smiles a little but not very much. When I'm a shrink, I'll know even more about body language. Oh yeah, I forgot to tell you. I'm not planning to work at the hotel forever. Soon as I save up enough money, I'm going to school to be a psychiatrist, a shrink. I didn't tell you about that but that's what I'm gonna do one of these days.

A friend of mine, another Quarter Rat, said his brother is a shrink; he said I'll need to go to medical school first if I want to do any shrinking. For now I'll just get a book that shrinks use and see what it means when you smile a little. I'm sure shrinks have to look up tons of garbage every day when you consider how nuts people are. Boy, who could keep up with that!

But it is true, I am super good at body language. You have to be to do what I do. If you're as good as I am you can look at someone and tell right away if they're confused. I'll give you a couple of clues. First, if you see someone staring at the sky you might think they're checking the weather, but they're not. People look at the sky when they're trying to figure something out. Like which way Bourbon Street is, for example. Or where Jackson Square is. It's like they expect the answer to be written in the sky by one of those planes that do that stuff. Remember those? You hardly see them anymore. Another thing they do is put their hands on their hips and stand perfectly still and look around. That's a real giveaway, but someone who isn't as skilled as I am would probably miss it.

There are tons more of these kinds of things. Sooner or later you get to know them all.

And me, when I'm at the hotel and see this I go over right away to help out. When you come right down to it, I'm already a lot like a shrink even though I'm not one.

But when Eddie smiles, you can't tell much. It's sort of like that smile on the person in the painting in the museum in France. You know the one I mean. The one where you can't figure out if she's happy or pissed off. My guess is pissed off. How would you feel if you sat there for hours and hours while the artist puts little specks of paint on the piece of canvas or whatever it is?

Well, Eddie's usually not pissed off. But you don't know if he's happy either. And I'm guessing Eddie's tome will be like that too, if he ever finishes it. No one will know if it's supposed to be a happy book or a sad book. My guess is some of both because that's the way Eddie is.

"I'm on chapter thirteen," Eddie suddenly says, like he knows I'm wondering.

Thirteen, that could be an unlucky chapter, I'm thinking.

But just then Eddie says, "I figure I'll be done in a year or two."

"That soon, huh?" Actually, I think that's way too long

even for a tome, but I don't tell him. Eddie's a very precise person. I'm sure that's why it's taking him so long. Here's what I think, Eddie wants every word to be in exactly the right place. You can tell he's a very precise person just sitting next to him right there in The Chart Room, for example. He always keeps his beer in exactly the same spot. Each time he takes a sip of beer and sets the glass down again he rearranges the coaster—you know, that little cardboard thingy they put on the bar to set your drink on—so that he's sure it's exactly where he wants. I'm serious…that's what he does. Even for someone like me who is pretty good at this shrink stuff, I have a little trouble figuring that one out. Some day if a shrink comes to the hotel (people love to tell you what they do for a living), I'll probably ask him what it means.

Eddie continues talking about the tome and then, wouldn't you know it, Horace Slagg comes crashing into The Chart Room. He's got this big grin stretched across his mug kind of like on a huge carp you dug up from the bottom of some bayou. Like I said, Horace is the total opposite of Eddie. Horace can't stop grinning and smiling no matter what. He even does it when he's talking. Sort of like that wooden puppet, Mortimer Snerd…remember him? I don't know if you've ever seen Mortimer Snerd. I remember seeing him on TV when I was a kid. A real doofus, let me tell you. He had a couple of buck teeth and all, and he always wore this silly straw hat and he'd sit on this guy's lap and the guy had one hand in a hole in Snerd's back so he could move the mouth up and down. And to make matters worse, Horace even wears one of those stupid straw hats now and then just like Snerd used to wear.

"Hey pal. Where's Sab?" Horace asks.

There he goes, the first thing out of Horace's mouth is: "Where's Sab?"

I just shrug. Boy, does that ever get people to shut up. I even do it at the hotel when I want someone to go away. They warn us, the dweebs, not to do it, not to shrug at people because it's sort of rude. But sometimes you just can't help it. Like when some dork asks you if it's gonna rain and it's already raining. No, I'm serious, people do crud like that all the time. I learned the shrugging thing from the bartender I know, and like I said, those guys are smart as hell, they know all the tricks.

Horace asks again, "So where's Sab?"

"Don't know…not my day to watch him," I finally say.

Horace grunts as if this is some tectonic tragedy. He ignores my answer and looks around the room to see if Sab might be hiding in the corner or something, waiting for a chance to slip away now that Horace has come in. Horace can be a real pest. Sab said he calls up all the time—I mean like ten, twenty times a day sometimes, and he always starts out the same: he says, "Hey pal, got something to tell ya." I guess he thinks that will be the hook that Sab can't resist, some real extraordinary secret that Horace is going to let Sab in one…just Sab and no one else. And then he proceeds to tell Sab about a new pair of shoes he bought or crap like that. He's probably hoping Sab's gonna say, "No shit, Horace, can I come by and take a look?" Or worse yet, Horace will say, "You gonna be in The Chart Room tonight, I'll show you them when I'm there." Needless to say, it's nothing but a trick to find out when Sab will be in The Chart Room so Horace can swing by and try to hitch up with one of Sab's women.

Well anyway, Horace is getting real impatient, which makes me hope he'll be leaving soon. God forbid if Sab comes in now because the night would be done for and I'd have to leave just to keep from puking while Horace tries to play Casanova.

But I've been around Horace enough to know that he'll be heading out soon. He has the patience of a cricket when things aren't going his way. And sure enough, his head bobbles around as he checks the room to see who's there one last time. Nobody there but us dweebs and Rats.

"If you see Sab, tell him I was here," Horace says.

"I'll get the memo out," I say.

Horace shuffles out, shifting this way and that as he walks in the frumpy way he has of doing it. His whole body kind of shakes to the left and then right and then back to left again like one of those old tall ships that they forgot to put ballast rocks in and is now blowing around like hell on the open ocean. I know quite a bit about that stuff, being from Baltimore and all and having once been down in the hold of one of those suckers. Well anyway, Horace swings his way out of The Chart Room—and not a second soon enough to my way of thinking.

6

Everything settles down pretty well once Horace is gone—bad vibes pour out of the guy. And guess what, not ten minutes later, Sab comes rolling into the bar. Big smile on his face, hands in his pocket. Sab always looks like he just won the lottery, and won real big. And he's got this blond hair that hangs loose, never combed but never messy. You've seen that kind of hair, I'm sure. And a nice blond beard, sort of like the old explorers used to have—the ones who traveled up and down the Amazon or across Africa or something like that. He looks real rugged but in a friendly kind of way. I'm sure that's why he's so hot to the women. Probably, women think explorers are real sexy. That's my guess.

Sab looks around the bar as he walks in. No doubt checking to see if Horace is here. I almost imagine that Sab was hunkered down outside knowing Horace would probably be in the bar, and then he came in once he saw Horace stumble out.

He sees me and Eddie and comes right over and sits down and orders a beer...a *Corona*. He always orders an imported beer, mostly Mexican ones. He likes *Corona*, but several others too. Some people look good when they drink imported beers. Others look like real dorks, Horace for example. And Horace always does this real dorky thing when he orders an imported beer. He takes a drink of it and then holds the beer in front of him and stares at the label like he's doing a commercial or something. I always want to grab the freakin' bottle from his hand and slam it down on the bar.

But Sab looks slick when he drinks imported beer. Kind of like that guy on TV who used to do the commercials, you know, the ones for *Dos Equis*. Remember him? Sab even looks like a young version of that guy. Much better looking, of course. And anyway, that guy was pretty damn old. I don't know why he had all those hot women hanging all over him. He's not on TV anymore. Most likely died, that's what I figure.

So, Sab starts telling us about his day working at the photography studio. It's on St. Charles Avenue below the French Quarter. Sab usually takes the streetcar to work and he always brings an extra shirt in the morning. The days are so hot you're drenched by noon. Let me tell you, I know all about that. Imagine what it's like wearing a monkey suit like I do all day. Well, the trick is to stay out of the sun and drink buckets of iced tea. I have this like two-gallon container of iced tea just inside the doors of the hotel so I can fill up from it whenever I want. And I have this big mug, you know like the kind with a handle on it. It's so big you need a handle just to pick the bugger up.

Sab tells us about the job he had for that day. He works

for a guy named Paul Poteet. The name of the studio is Poteet Photography. Not very original but he's been in business a long time and all the snooty old farts in New Orleans go to him to get their mug shots taken—that's what Sab calls the portraits.

Sab and Poteet don't get along so well, which is unusual because Sab is a real easy-going dude. But Sab and Poteet are like oil and water. Sab calls him Popeye…well, you know, not to his face, but Sab says he looks a lot like Popeye. I've never seen this Poteet guy but Sab says he's got this kind of round nose and a big chin like Popeye had. And to make matters worse he has these pumped-up Popeye-like arms. Remember how Popeye had those big fat forearms? Oh yeah, and just like Popeye he squints and looks out of one eye a lot…and he mumbles a lot when he's working.

Sab said a couple of times he almost called him Popeye to his face. That would have gone over real well I bet! *Mamma Mia!* They were working one day and Sab said, "Hey Popeye, while you're over there can you pick up one of those extension cords?"

So anyway, Sab and Popeye are always arguing about how to set up a "shoot". That's what Sab calls it, "a shoot". Sab wants super elaborate lighting. Popeye mumbles that it's a waste of time. Says these people might have barrels of money but they're dumb as a bedpost…wouldn't know Einstein from a beer stein, that's what Popeye always says. And he's probably right. That would certainly describe the people who come to the hotel wearing the real expensive rags. Especially the people who are throwing money around like it's that fake crap you get in a Monopoly game. The ones who stick a big bill in your hand and close your hand so you won't lose it, like I mentioned earlier. Or the ones who stick the money in your pants pocket and pat it to make sure it won't fall out. (Sometimes women do that. Men never do…thank you!)

Sab tells us he had this big shoot outside in the park. It was a wedding and everyone from the wedding party was dressed-to-the-nines. And to make it worse the day was hotter than a sputtering grease pan and the bride was dripping wet and her makeup was running and the big expensive hairdo she had kept sagging and then she started crying because of it all. And Sab was trying to be cheery. He said he smiled a lot but it made him look like he was laughing at her and that made the whole crappy thing even worse.

"By the end of the day I felt like I'd been dragged through a knothole," Sab says as he heads into his second *Corona* in less than five minutes. "I know Popeye did this to me on purpose…dumped this job on me while he sat in an air-conditioned studio doing mug shots of the uptown battleaxes!"

So, while he's telling us this, one of Sab's girlfriends comes into The Chart Room. I've seen her a couple of times. Her name is Joey. She's wearing this red dress, I mean the shortest thing you ever saw. It comes all the way up to…well, you get the picture. I can tell you, there are a lot of Rats in The Chart Room that nearly choke the minute they see her.

She's got this thick wavy hair that's sort of rust-brown and the biggest brown eyes you've ever seen. And not a lick of makeup on. See, now that's the thing about real good-looking women, they don't need makeup. You should see the women who come to the hotel, the ones wearing the real expensive rags, the ones I just talked about. You might think they look real good but they've always got this makeup pancaked onto their face. And they have this sort of bright yellow hair that's stacked all over the place on top of their head. And big monster pieces of jewelry, too. I mean they look like little cast-iron skillets hanging from their earlobes or whatever.

Joey sits on a stool next to Sab, and he orders a drink for her. I'm not sure what he ordered…gin and tonic maybe. He seems to know exactly what everyone of his women like. It's a real skill, a real art, keeping track of it all. I could never do it. I'm sure it makes them all feel real special. And Joey is a very friendly person. She takes a tiny sip of the drink and tosses her hair back over her head and rakes her fingers through her hair. She does this a lot and it makes her look great. You would think she's a model of some kind but Sab told me she's a lawyer. He met her when he was doing mug shots for the law firm she works for. She turns toward Sab and crosses her legs and you can imagine what that does to her dress, short as it is already. Egads!

And now Rats of all kinds are beginning to buzz like hornets. They try to make it not too obvious, but you can tell plain as can be what they're up to. They march past us as if they're just heading to the john but they always check out Joey as they go past. Really now, this many people don't need to take a leak all at once. Though it is true that with all the beer and hurricanes everyone drinks in the Quarter, and all the heat and all, people are always making trips to the john. At the hotel, for example, horse-buggies like Eddie drives are always pulling over to let some someone out for an emergency trip inside. You can tell exactly what's going on from the look on their face as they tack their way into the hotel lobby at warp speed.

So, it's a steady stream of Rats, one after another, past Joey. Joey ignores them…she's probably used to it. She starts asking Sab about his photography. She likes to talk about it and I know Sab's done some shoots with her just for the hell of it because he's got some great pics of her on the wall in his apartment.

You can see how easy it would be to work with her because she looks great from every direction. That's probably a real challenge if you're a photographer—finding the perfect angle to take the picture from. Horace always says it takes a lot of skill and he says how good Sab is at it. I know Horace is just trying to suck up to Sab when he says that even though it is true about how much skill Sab has. Horace will do any crappy little thing he can think of to get Sab's attention, like telling him he's got these way-cool shoes that Sab needs to see…remember? One time he actually did come into The Chart Room wearing the shoes just to prove he has them I think. They were bright red wingtips, the kind with those little holes on the top of the toes, and they were real shiny suckers. They looked like Horace had spent two days polishing the shit out of them just to make them look that way…no, I'm totally serious!

Eddie and I just sit there while Joey talks. It's hard to say much of anything without losing your train of thought when you're next to her. I feel like telling Eddie she'd be a great character for his tome but his book is so long already it's probably chock-full of people like Joey. How else can you make a book that big?

I heard that when you write a tome you need to put a lot of people in it so that it's real difficult for readers to keep up with them all. That's why they study tomes in English Lit classes, because they're so huge and the professors can kill a whole semester with just one tome, and it might even be the only book the guy ever read, and so they end up with a lot of time to play golf or go bowling or whatever professors do with all the time they have. And I'm sure they have a lot of time when you consider they're only in the classroom for like maybe an hour a day.

I heard it's real hard to get one of those professor jobs because you have to know your stuff even if you read only one crappy book. That's what I heard.

Every now and then one of these guys, these professor guys, comes into the hotel. You can spot them right away because they always wear these tweed sport coats even in the middle of summer. And the coats always have leather patches on the elbows. It's a dead give-away.

Well, Sab tells Joey he's taking a couple of days off. You should see her eyes sparkle.

"Popeye's been working me to death," he tells her. And then he tells her about his afternoon shoot, the outdoor wedding, and how the bride had a total meltdown in the middle of it.

Joey makes this cute little wiggle and crosses her legs again to the other side. She tries to pull her dress down but it's no use, it's about as high up as it can be without getting us kicked out of the bar for perverting the minds of Quarter Rats. And this is New Orleans, mind you. A place where at Mardi Gras women flop their jugs around for a lousy string of plastic beads and guys strut through the Quarter in jock straps with shiny sequins sewn onto them and the gay dudes go around and pinch each other's nipples when they pass one of their pals because, you see, they're not wearing anything but that dinky jock strap like I just mentioned. And, let me tell you, they swivel their hips a lot, and I mean a *lot*.

Joey says to Sab, "So, when are you taking off? We can take a trip together. Maybe along the Gulf Coast over in Mississippi. It's real nice there."

See how easy it is for Sab to score. He didn't do anything except say he's taking a day or two off and Joey's already got a trip planned. I suspect she wants to be sure she gets in on the action while she can.

And she is right about the Gulf Coast over in Mississippi being nice. I was there once. Problem was, I got my ass bit by a real mean crab or one of those slimy jelly fish that sneak up on you when you're not looking. Holy cow, my butt puffed up like an inner tube and I could barely sit on it for a whole rotten week.

Sab says something to Joey but I can't hear what he says.

I try hard without making it too obvious, but he talks sort of low. I figure if I can hear what he says I might be able to use it sometime if I ever need to. It's good to have answers stored up so you don't have to fumble around. Anyway, whatever he says, it must've been the right answer because Joey's eyes get real big and she smiles this nice smile.

I think I forgot if I told you about her smile. It's like you see on those TV commercials of people for the fancy toothpaste. The stuff that costs a couple of bucks just for one tube. Me, I use *Ipana*…it's been around a hell of a long time and I figure if it's good enough for old Bucky Beaver it's good enough for me. It used to come in this yellow and red tube, but now it's in a white tube to make it look more fancy, I guess.

Same thing with shampoo. Have you seen how many kinds there are in the drugstores now? I use *Prell*. But it's hard to get these days so when I see it in the store I usually buy ten or twenty bottles at once so I won't run out. I almost have a small closet full of the stuff. One day it got so hot in my apartment one of the tubes exploded and there was shampoo junk everywhere. It made the whole place smell like Prell for about a week. I didn't mind though because my apartment is so small you only have to clean it about maybe once every couple of months or so. And anyway, most of the dirt and dust has been smashed into the floors and cracks and you'll never get it out no matter how hard you try.

Well anyway, Joey has this real neat smile. She gets these dimples on her cheeks when she smiles. You've probably seen people like that. The dimples are sort of hidden. You don't see them until they smile and then there they are just like that. It's how it is with Joey.

Joey crosses her legs again to the other side and the temperature in The Chart Room is going way up from all the huffing of the Rats.

7

I stay at The Chart Room for a long time, mostly just chewing the fat with Eddie Clabberman. Longer than I probably should have but it's my day off and I feel like drinking beer, especially after the sausage PoBoy and Mr. Pibb I had for lunch. That's the trick with those. You can eat one and six hours later you feel like you just ate it because they're packed with protein. I mean packed! Probably as much protein as you would get in a chocolate milkshake with one of those maraschino cherries on it like they serve at the fast-food joints.

It's late when I leave The Chart Room. I go home and climb in bed…more like fall in bed. I don't move all night long and the next thing I know my alarm clock is ringing. I climb out of bed. Boy do I feel bad. Like I got clobbered with a big stick, or like the time a suitcase fell off the top of a taxi and landed smack on my head.

I'm thinking about going over to the free clinic in the Quarter. It's a place that most of the Quarter Rats go to. It's got this real hip doctor. He looks like he's straight out of the sixties. He's got this long hair that hangs down on the sides of his head and in the back all the way to his shoulders but the top of his head is totally bald. He always wears a nice shirt, mostly plaid, and no tie and he hangs his stethoscope around his neck the way all the docs do. They probably teach them that in medical school. He's a real cool guy and he sure knows his stuff though his hands are a little shaky. Sometimes I'm kinda worried that if he ever has to give me a shot, like a tetanus shot to keep me from getting lockjaw and having to suck up my dinner through a straw until my jaw unlocks, that he'll miss my arm and shoot the stuff right into his own hand.

It's ten-thirty, sort of later than I usually get up but I don't start working until four o'clock so I got lots of time to screw around a bit or do nothing or whatever I feel like.

I pick up my phone and see that Ramona left a message. She says she's gonna put my shoes—the ones I took to the cobbler and left at her house—by the back door of her apartment if I want to come by and pick them up. Actually, I feel like no one would steal them because they look like roadkill even though they don't feel like it when you wear them. But it is true, there are lots of Quarter Rats who would love to have a pair as good as these.

So I swing by Ramona's and grab the shoes and head over to the café and order a cup of coffee and a quiche from Franka and go sit in the courtyard out back. Cripes it's nice out! I feel pretty good even with the lousy hangover I have.

Soon as the coffee arrives I drink about half of it and then lean back and just breath the air. The courtyard has these jasmine flowers that smell like a million. It's like the best thing in the world.

It's not long before Clifford Ritter comes rolling into the café. Funny, he's usually in here earlier but somehow it's like he knows I'm here. It's okay, I don't mind. Clifford's one of the nicer Rats but he can get annoying with the way he has of describing stuff. I think I told you about that yesterday.

He orders a latte and beignets, like always, and starts telling me about his trip over to Algiers.

"Took the ferry," he garbles, with a chunk of beignet in his mouth. "Doesn't take long, about half an hour. Wanna hear something crazy? There was almost nobody on the ferry. It got me a little worried because it usually takes about fifteen minutes to get the cars and people on. So I was pretty worried there was something wrong with the ferry and they weren't telling us. Like maybe there was a hole in the side or something, and they had patched it and they weren't telling us. But I got on anyway."

It's possible Clifford has a point. The ferry is usually almost filled at midday.

"So when I saw that, I made sure I was standing next to one of those lifesavers they string on the side of the ferry…you know, the white ones. It seems to me like these ferries could tip over pretty easy with all the weight from the cars and stuff. Then you'd have to hang onto a lifesaver while you're floating around in the Mississippi. And the worst thing about it is, what about the sharks? You don't hear much about the sharks," Clifford says, "but I bet there are tons of them in the river. It's just that you can't see them because the water's so muddy."

There aren't any sharks in the Mississippi. I know this for a fact, being from Baltimore and knowing a lot about water from living near the Chesapeake Bay. There aren't any sharks in the Chesapeake Bay, either—you know there aren't when you consider how many blue crabs there are in the Bay. I mean the place is filled with them. If there were sharks in the Bay the crabs would be wiped out by now. Think how easy it would be for a shark to snatch up a crab. Of course it's always possible that sharks don't like crabs, or that crabs make sharks puke. I used to love crabs. I'd eat dozens of them steamed in Old Bay seasoning. But then one day I ate so many I thought *I* was gonna puke.

"Well, we made it over to Algiers okay, and the ferry didn't tip over or nothing…not this time at least. I didn't go the record shop like I planned, the one with all the vinyl. Instead, I went to a music store that sells used stuff like used guitars and I even saw an old French horn, if you can believe it. But it looked in pretty good shape. I tried puffing on it, but nothing came out. Anyway, I found a real great used guitar," Clifford says. "It barely cost forty dollars, though one of the strings is busted. See, what I'm planning to do is to play music in Jackson Square. Some of those guys out there really haul in the bread."

And you know, of course, Clifford has to give you all the details of everything.

"I saw this guy. Cripes, he must've had around fifty bucks or so right there in front of him. Some of them only get coins and a few bills but there're always a couple of bubbas that really clean up. You know who do best of all?"

He waits as if I'm gonna ask who. But I don't and so he says, "The violin players, that's who. Especially the Asian ones, or the ones who look Asian anyway. Wow, people pack up close to hear them. But I'm pretty good with the guitar. And I've got a little trick up my sleeve that's gonna help. See, what I'll do is play lots of junk about N.O. The tourists will eat that shit up. For example, one of the songs I'll play is *Mr. Bojangles.* Remember that one? And I'll do this totally cool thing. At the end I'll jump way up in the air and click my heels like *Bojangles* used to do. Here, watch."

He gets up to show me what he means. He jumps as high as he can, like two feet off the ground, and tries to click his heels but it doesn't go so well and he ends up on his butt.

"Still working on it," he says, dusting himself off. "I've been practicing in my apartment. It's not quite there but it's coming. Maybe tomorrow I'll show you."

Can't wait.

Clifford sits down again and digs into his beignets. He's got powdered sugar all over his fingertips, which he licks off instead of using his napkin. He doesn't say anything for a quite a while. He's probably feeling real stupid from the *Bojangles* thing. I sure would. He tears through his beignets pretty quick and sucks up most of his latte to wash them down. His fingertips are finally all clean, but he wipes his them on his pants just to be sure…I suppose.

I ask him if he's gonna give up being a hack…when he starts his gig in Jackson Square.

He thinks about it, doesn't answer. He shrugs and shakes

his head. I guess that's a no…might be, not sure.

My shoes, the ones I got over at Ramona's are sitting on the chair next to me. Clifford sees them and picks one up. I'm a little worried he's gonna get powdered sugar all over it, but it seems like he licked most of the stuff off his fingers.

"Now *this* is a good shoe," Clifford says. He turns it over. "Yikes, the soles aren't even worn…not a bit. That's a good sign."

"Had new soles put on," I say.

Clifford nods as if he approves. "Wanna hear something crazy?" he says.

Here we go.

"One time, I had a pair of shoes…sort of like these." He holds the shoe up and shakes it a little, kind of like for emphasis. Any real good shrink could tell you why people do that, I'm sure.

I'm hoping he's not gonna mess with the shoes too much because the last thing I need to do today is clean lumps of powdered sugar off them. I'm not a clean-freak or anything like that, because I don't clean my apartment all that much, like I already mentioned, but I like stuff to be just right. Like at the hotel. I hate it when my red coat gets wrinkled. They're supposed to send it off to get cleaned but they almost never do. And it's probably one of the reasons Ramona and I get along so well, both of us being real particular how we look. Like yesterday when she was doing her runway walk thing with her new clothes, the stuff she just bought, you could tell what a super neat person she is when it comes to clothes.

Clifford is still inspecting the shoes. He never gets around to telling me the crazy thing. Which I'm happy as hell for. Instead, he says, "Going to the flea market over on Peters Street or maybe the one on Magazine. One of them…not sure which."

Now he starts telling me about each one, and a few others too. Like which flea market is better and which is worse. And I'm thinking, does it really matter…really, Clifford? Gads, I mean flea markets are flea markets, so what's the deal?

"I need a new guitar string. And I'm looking for a shirt to wear on my gig, you know, when I play in Jackson Square. I need something that's sort of faded so I look like I'm real desperate."

Shouldn't be too hard to do.

"That's when people give the most. When they think you barely have enough food to eat. But you don't want something with holes in it or nothing like that or they're gonna think you're a hobo."

Hobo?

"So, the trick is to get just the right shirt. And flea markets have lots of them and some are real cheap. Like a buck or two. And sometimes you can even weasel the guy down to fifty cents if you're good at that sort of thing."

I'm thinking: how about not splattering what you eat all over your clothes and face, that might help when it comes to getting tips. If you've got food all over you they'll know you're not exactly starving.

Clifford starts telling me more about the shirt when Sab

and Joey come into the café. Boy does Joey look good! Even better than last night. Sab looks great, too. You can bet they had a wild night. Any shrink could tell that instantly just from looking at them. That's the thing about shrinks, they know a lot about people just by looking at them. Of course, they have to stare real hard and not let you know they're staring. It's tricky. I'm good at it…I have to be when you consider what I do all day at the hotel. If you try telling someone a joke and they're in a big pissed off mood let's say, you just wasted a good joke for no reason because they're not gonna laugh no matter how funny it is. In fact, they'll probably give you this real mean pissed-off groan and walk away.

"We're going over to the Mississippi Coast for a couple of days," Sab says.

Joey has a big smile. The dimples pop out on her cheeks like I talked about last night. The ones that only show up when she smiles. You can tell she's super happy.

"Need to have you get my mail and put it in the apartment," Sab says, "if you don't mind."

"You betcha," I say, making it sound like I'm from Minnesota or North Dakota or one of those places way up north.

He hands me the key. "New shoes?" he asks, picking one up.

"Naw, those are Rubin's old shoes. He got new leather put on the bottom," Clifford explains right away. "Pretty good stuff, huh? No roadkill or nothing."

Sab smiles and puts the shoe on the chair again. "*Ciao!*"

he says, and they head out.

That's another thing about Sab. He knows all kinds of languages. He even knows French. See, a lot of people who come to Popeye's for photos know French, so Sab has to know how to talk to them. Sometimes when we're all out at The Chart Room some of his French will slip out. For example, instead of saying Cheers or something like that when he holds up his beer for a toast, lots of times he says *à votre santé*. I have no idea what it means, but he says it a lot. Every now and then Horace Slagg uses it too. Remember Horace? But it sounds real phony when he does it. And you know Horace is the kind of dorky Rat who will do anything to impress people. Especially Sab's girlfriends.

So, Joey swings around and out they go—off to Mississippi.

Okay now, Clifford is back to talking about his plans to start doing his gig in Jackson Square. "You have to know the routine," he says. "It's real dog-eat-dog out there. You want to get there early or you won't get a good spot, and you have to watch out not to take a spot that someone else always uses. Let me tell you, that really ticks them off." He explains that he saw a couple of Rats practically get into a brawl over it. "They're super territorial in Jackson Square. They aren't always so nice to each other when it comes to junk like that. Dog-eat-dog world...that's what it is." He takes his finger and rubs it across the beignet plate and scoops up a little powdered sugar and licks his finger.

I pick up my shoes and set them on the floor next to me

away from Clifford.

But he is right about Rats looking out for their turf in Jackson Square. I know this guy, his name is Jim Yute, he's a painter and all he does is paint clowns. I think I mentioned those kinds of painters a while back, the dudes that paint only clowns. Well, they don't do all that well. Maybe sell like one or two paintings a day. All day for a couple of lousy bucks.

The Rats that really sell their stuff are the ones that put little dabs of paint on a speck at a time. And it helps if you paint stuff like St. Louis Cathedral because it's right there in Jackson Square and people watch the painter and then say, "Geez, look at that, Helen, he's painting the church…and it really looks like it too!" And they all turn and look at the church and then at his painting again. And usually those painters have lots of paintings like that hanging on the fence where they're working and most of the paintings are super expensive…like at least a hundred bucks or so. It's probably worth it though, because they're so good that if you didn't see them doing it you'd never know they actually painted it and that it's not one of those paint-by-numbers jobs. I think there are a few Rats out there who try to peddle paint-by-numbers jobs. I like to get up real close to the painting to see if I can see the numbers under the paint. They get real fried when they see you doing it, though.

Actually, most of the painters that do well are pretty old. Or that's what it seems like, anyway, because they always have this silvery hair, even the women. It makes them look like they've been doing this painting thing for a long time and that they really got it figured out now. I heard it takes longer to be a painter than to be a shrink. I don't really believe it but that's what I heard.

Well anyway, Jim Yute never makes much money. I'm thinking maybe he doesn't look old enough to be a good painter, and if he bought some hair dye to make his hair look gray he'd do better. I always feel kinda sorry for him. I hear him push his cart with all his painting gear down the street early in the morning so he can get the same spot and not have some asshole Rat jump on him for taking his spot.

He sometimes comes to The Chart Room and has a beer, but mostly he just buys a six pack and drinks it at home. Once I stopped by to see him. He lives in a place close to me—it's even smaller than mine. When he opened the door it was almost dark inside. He had a candle burning because the city turned off his electricity. He was eating cold Campbell's Pork & Beans out of the can. You would think Jim would be super depressed all the time but he almost never is. He always has a good outlook on life. I don't see how he pulls it off, but when I'm a shrink I'll have enough time to think about stuff like that. Right now I'm way too busy to give it much thought.

Clifford pulls a watch from his pocket. A silver pocket watch with a top that flips up. He's had the thing for years. I think he got it at one of the flea markets. I remember him telling me that. He snaps the top shut and stuffs it into his pocket and just sits there for a while doing nothing.

"Thought you had to go over to the flea market," I say.

"I'm fixin' to," he answers.

There you go, that's one of his favorite phrases…fixin' to. I don't get it. If you're fixin' to, just go do it. You can see how Clifford can drive you a little nuts at times.

"Don't want to wait till all the good stuff at the market is picked over," he adds. He pulls his watch out and checks the time again. Of course, it's about the same time as when he looked at it thirty seconds ago.

Franka comes by and asks if we want anything else. I'm thinking, oh cripes, Clifford isn't fixin' to get another batch of beignets, is he? See, that's another thing about Clifford, he gets all hopped up to do something and then putzes around for a long time before he does it. Way too much fixin' to, in my opinion.

Imagine if I was like that at the hotel. So, someone says, "Hey Bub, wanna grab that bag over there for me?" And I say I'm fixin' to…I'm fixin' to. And then maybe I check the time on my watch or whatever. Imagine that. Well, Clifford does crud like that all the time. I'm wondering if he'll ever get around to doing his gigs in Jackson Square. My bet is no.

He tells Franka he's fine—no more beignets this morning.

Boy am I relieved. For one thing all that sugar isn't so good for you. When I'm a shrink, I'm gonna warn people about it because I think it's a big reason people go crazy. I mean, look at Clifford, for example. Okay, he's not crazy, not too much. Me? I hardly ever eat that much sugar, except for a Snickers bar about once a week. That's probably what I'll tell my patients…stick with Snickers bars. My guess is, if I open a psychiatry office in N.O., I'm gonna get gobs of people who are addicted to beignets. At least I won't go broke.

Clifford checks his watch for the third time and then believe it or not he gets up and leaves. I get the feeling he doesn't really want to go to the flea market. Besides, most of his shirts are faded as hell and pretty worn out. So I don't see why he needs to buy more. Just wear the crap you already have.

I meant to ask him if he got a guitar case with the used guitar he bought over in Algiers. It's important so people will have a place to toss in all the loot he's expecting to get. Could always get himself an old top hat instead, I suppose. You can probably get one at the flea market real cheap. They have all kinds of useless garbage at those places or else they wouldn't call it a flea markets. In fact, it's probably the reason they call it a flea market in the first place. I mean what would you do with a bunch of lousy fleas?

If I see Clifford tomorrow I'll ask about the guitar case. The top hats are more for the mimes and magicians…that kind of crap. I doubt that Clifford's thought this through very well. You can see how complicated it all is if you want to do it right. And he sure as hell needs to work on that *Bojangles* thing or next thing you know they'll be carting him off to Charity Hospital with a busted tush. Tush, a stupid word but my mother used to use it all the time back in Baltimore. They'll have to cart Clifford off to Charity for sure because a busted tush is not something you can get fixed at a free clinic or wherever. You bust your tush and you're gonna need a specialist, someone who really knows his stuff…a proctologist most likely.

I'm getting ready to leave but figure I'll hang out for a couple more minutes…the night at The Chart Room took a lot out of me.

Then, this guy comes into the café. He's got *The New Orleans Times-Picayune* tucked under his arm and a camera hanging from his shoulder. He sits at a table a little farther from me. Franka comes by and talks to him for a second and calls him Mr. Poteet.

Holy cow, here he is! Popeye! In the flesh! And sure enough he looks exactly like Sab always says—got those giant forearms and all. He orders something, I can't tell what because he kind of mumbles just like Popeye used to do. Remember…in the cartoons and all, the ways Sab described?

I'm thinking any minute now Bluto's gonna come busting his way into the café and grab Popeye by the neck or something. And next thing you know, Popeye will yank a can of spinach from his pocket and squeeze it and the spinach will squirt up in the air and come down right in Popeye's mouth, a perfect shot. By the way, have you ever tasted spinach that comes out of a can. It's absolutely disgusting. Not even green, kind of grey and real revolting. Sorta smells bad, too. My mother used to give us that junk when I was growing up in Baltimore. She told us it would make us just like Popeye. Terrific, just what I wanted.

So, Popeye's reading the newspaper. I'm keeping an eye on him real secret like. He's reading the paper and every couple of minutes he mumbles something. I can't make out what he's saying—that's the thing with Popeye in the cartoons, you can never understand a single word. So he keeps reading and mumbling off and on.

Franka comes by and starts talking to him. He says something but I only get part of it…I hear him say, "Oh shua, honey. D'jah hee-yah what they's plannin' ta do in Naw-lins?"

Well, I'm not as good at languages as Sab, but all my experience at the hotel tells me right away Popeye is a N.O native. Probably been here his whole life.

Franka nods and Popeye returns to the newspaper. Me, I've pretty much had enough of all of this for today. I get up and leave.

8

I start down Toulouse Street. As I pass Jackson Square, I figure I'll check around and see what's happening and give Clifford a report if I see him tomorrow. Mostly, I'm looking for open spots where none of the other Rats are working. And you have to be sure you're not too close to another musician. If you're playing *Mr. Bojangles* and the Rat next to you is playing something real cool on the fiddle...well, you get the picture. I'm not sure who wrote *Mr. Bojangles* but you can be pretty damn sure it wasn't Beethoven.

So I wander around Jackson Square checking out all the places where Clifford could start doing his gigs. When I get over where *Café du Monde* is I get creamed by a family coming out of the restaurant. They all look like they had way too much sugar, especially the guy who's probably the father. He looks like he ate about two dozen beignets all by himself not to mention how many the rest of the family packed down.

I try to move away but he's coming at about four hundred miles an hour, and he's not looking. I make this fast move like the skinny football players do when they're tearing down the field for a TD, but he's like a refrigerator that you can't get around and, of course, we collide…like big time.

I want to get pissed off, but I have to admit, the guy is pretty nice and he seems to feel real bad. He helps me get up and asks if I'm okay. He needs to lay off the sugar, I'm thinking. But I don't say it because he seems pretty honest and all.

Let me tell you, if you're a Quarter Rat you take your life in your hands just going anywhere near Jackson Square. Last thing I need is a visit to see Doc Mellman at the free clinic—or worse, over to Charity Hospital with a busted tush.

I make it the rest of the way around the Square with no other near-death experiences. As I get near St. Louis Cathedral I see Jim Yute. He's looking good for someone who barely makes a penny.

"Rubin!" he calls, as I walk up.

He's sitting on a stool painting a picture of a clown's face on this square cardboard-looking thing. It's sort of a happy clown but you can't tell for sure. That's the deal with clowns, they put all that face paint on to make them look happy and sad both. Jim seems to know all about it. I'm wondering if he was a clown once. Maybe in the circus probably.

He's got a can of Mr. Pibb next to him. He seems to like this Mr. Pibb junk. I never see him drinking anything else. I can take one now and then but that's about it.

He starts telling me about how great the morning has been. "Two paintings…almost forty dollars! Man, if I can keep this up I'm gonna be rolling in bucks," he says. "Thought it might rain today." He looks up at the sky. "Still might."

Jim keeps this big tarp on his cart so he can cram his paintings underneath if it starts to pour. And in N.O. it can pour at any time. At the hotel we keep a lot of umbrellas inside, and let me tell you, you walk someone to a cab and hold an umbrella for them, you can count on a super-good tip. That's why I don't mind the rain. But in the Square, the Rats hate it. No one's gonna play a fiddle in the rain, that's for sure. You do that and the things gonna get soggy and warp up like a pretzel. Same thing for Clifford's guitar even if it was a used one with a busted string that he bought over in Algiers.

"Whatcha doing over here?" Jim asks. He knows I hate coming to Jackson Square.

I tell him about Clifford. Then I tell him about getting creamed by the guy coming out of *Café du Monde*. While I'm talking, I check to make sure my clothes and shoes are clean—I hate it when I get the scum from the flagstones on me. That stuff is like bubblegum—you step on it and can't get it off the bottom of your shoe.

I'm hoping Jim will sell at least one more clown today. I don't know how many clowns you have to sell to have a big day…at least three would be my guess, especially when you consider how bad inflation is these days and how the cost of stuff like Campbell's Pork & Beans has probably skyrocketed.

As I head out of the Square I pass a mime. This is a different kind of mime—you start to see a lot of them these days. It's the new thing for Rats to do. They try to pretend they're a statue and not even alive or anything. Their whole body and all their clothes are all done up in shiny metallic paint…usually silver or gold. Some of them even try to look like some hot-shot person like Abraham Lincoln, or maybe like the Statue of Liberty. And the trick is they don't move a muscle. I mean nothing. They don't even blink. Not sure how they pull it off. You wouldn't think people would want to stop and watch someone doing nothing, would you? My guess is they stare at them for a long time to see if they're gonna blink.

And there's always one of them that pretends he's sitting on a chair but there's no chair there. They're kind of bent over like you'd be if you were sitting down. Most people can't figure this one out. They even walk to the side to see if they can find the trick. Like maybe the guy has a hidden stool you can't see…something like that.

I know a Rat who is one of those mimes in Jackson Square. He comes into The Chart Room a lot. He's actually pretty normal looking and he's not bent over or crunched up so you know it's not something weird that's wrong with him. Next time I see him I'm gonna ask what the trick is. But he might not tell me because you have to be real careful what you tell people about your mime secrets so they don't start blabbing it around the Quarter and screw up their schtick. I like that word. A friend of mine used to use it back in Baltimore. I think it's a Jewish word, I'm not real sure. I'll ask Sab sometime. He uses it a lot, and a bunch of other words like chutzpah…oh, yeah, and mazel tov, too.

I start down St. Ann Street toward my apartment. I pass by Sab's place but there's no point in checking the mail since the mailman doesn't deliver until the afternoon in the Quarter. I'm pretty certain they hate coming to the Quarter because it's filled with drunks and tourists and Quarter Rats...and Cajuns, too.

Some of my friends are Cajuns. At first I couldn't understand a word they said, but now I'm getting pretty good at it and I even speak a little Cajun myself. Sab's real good at it. But like I said, he speaks a whole bunch of languages. Cajuns talk real strange, kind of like if you ran all the words together in one huge long sentence. I'm sure there's some professor in one of those English Lit departments somewhere who specializes in Cajun. I bet they even bring Cajuns in to speak to the students just to prove people really speak Cajun and to show them how difficult it is to figure out what they're actually saying.

Well, down here in N.O. lots of people talk Cajun. I even hear it a lot at the hotel. In fact, one of our bartenders is a Cajun. His name is Remy. I heard it's a common Cajun name. They like to use names that no one else uses. He has this wavy black hair and he really knows his drinks...wow! I already told you bartenders have to be real smart. They have to keep track of all the buttons on the cash registers so they can ring up the bar tab just right, sorta like what astronauts do when they push all those buttons on the screens in the spaceships or whatever. It's a hell of a big deal.

When I get to my apartment the AC is working overtime, but it's not too bad inside. The thing with the mime is still bugging me. I'm wondering if I might be able to do it to pick up a few extra bucks. So I try doing this thing where you stand super still and don't move a bit. I mean not even breathing or blinking at all. If I do this I'll have to be someone famous that none of the other Rats are doing. I don't know who that would be—it would take some real hard thinking. One possibility might be someone like Richard Nixon. I'd have to fix my nose a bit. But he's not a real good choice because lots of people didn't like him and I don't want anyone puking right there in front of me. I wasn't too crazy about the guy either.

I guess I could be someone real corny like Mickey Mouse. And the good thing about that is I could get some big yellow shoes and fill them with sand so I can lean sideways and not even fall over. Nah, not Mickey Mouse.

Okay, now I got it...Charlie Chaplin. There used to be a Rat who did Charlie Chaplin, but I haven't seen him in a long while. Not sure where he went. Some big rich movie guy from Hollywood probably saw him and gave him a job in the movie business and he's probably a famous actor now. That's the thing about being a Rat in N.O., you never know who's gonna come strolling by, like when Jim Nabors came by The Chart Room that time.

I could go to one of the flea markets and get a crappy old black suit like Charlie Chaplin used to wear and get a cane and one of those frumpy hats with a round top. And one of those stubby mustaches, sort of like what Hitler had. I'll just get a fake one and stick it on. And some white gloves. Never figured out why a tramp wore gloves, and white ones at that. And the best thing is, I wouldn't have to stand still for hours and hours.

I could just walk back and forth and swing the cane like he did. And do that loony walk like he did—you know, the penguin sort of thing. I think you can see already how good I am at coming up with great ideas. You learn a lot working as a bellhop at the hotel. I mean you have to really know how to think on your feet. And sometimes fast as hell. I don't think Clifford is so hot at thinking. I mean look how much he still needs to do to get his gig rolling and even then it might be a total flop.

That's the problem with a lot of the Quarter Rats. Most are barely getting by. So even if you got a crappy job like I do, having to dress up like a monkey and all, it's not so bad when you come right down to it. And look at Ramona—she makes more in an hour than Jim Yute probably makes all day, more like two days. But then Ramona is a real classy dresser, like when she wears those seersucker shorts she showed me yesterday, the skimpy little blue and white ones. Were those rad or what? You can be sure it drives all the geezers nuts at the bar she works at, just like last night when Joey was at The Chart Room.

I decide to try doing a Charlie Chaplin imitation. I walk around in front of this mirror I have. If I remember, Charlie Chaplin's feet pointed way apart, like in opposite directions. And he waddled a lot. I give it a try. Well, it's actually pretty easy because you waddle when your feet are pointed apart. I think this is gonna be cinch and I figure people are gonna load me up with lots of loot as soon as they see me doing my Chaplin thing.

But I need more room to practice it. Apartments in the Quarter are pretty damn small so I go outside and down to the courtyard. I'm out there waddling around and Virginia starts up the stairs. You probably don't remember Virginia, she has an apartment near mine. She was heading out when I was coming home the other night, remember? Doesn't matter. But she sees me and comes over and asks how I am. She thinks I hurt my legs or something and can't walk.

I laugh pretty loud and say, "No, I'm walking like Charlie Chaplin."

"Like who?"

"Charlie Chaplin. The guy who made all those dumb old-time movies." I can see she doesn't know who I'm talking about.

"Oh," she says, and goes up the stairs.

I keep this routine up for a while. I'm getting pretty good at it actually, especially the thing where I kick my leg up the way Charlie Chaplin used to do when he started walking down the road. Remember that? But it is a little exhausting even for someone like me who's not old or worn-out or anything.

I feel like I need a little energy, though, so I go to the store on the corner to get a box of Milk Duds. The things are great. Full of energy. Even better than Snicker's bars. I have a box of Milk Duds almost every day. If I don't have a Snickers bar, that is. And even though the store on the corner is sort of dingy and dark and dirty and kind of creepy, they always have Milk Duds.

Sometimes I get a box of Milk Duds there and sometimes

a bottle of Mr. Pibb, but boy you do *not* want to have them together. I mean *that's* like lethal. All that sugar...geemanee! The next thing you know you're over at Doc Mellman's getting your stomach pumped. I never had my stomach pumped but it doesn't sound like a whole bunch of fun. I guess they hook you up to some sort of vacuum cleaner like thing...not real sure, but don't want to find out.

So, I'm standing in the store and...oh yeah, the place is called *Git n' Scram*. They sell everything you can think of. And I mean everything! Food, mostly canned junk. Probably even canned spinach. And tobacco and pipes—some real fancy ones, too. Like the one Sherlock Holmes used. And they sell cigarettes. The place kind of smells like tobacco. And they sell cold drinks and lots and lots of candy bars. And even some clothes. Like you can get T-shirts with pictures of Bourbon Street on them, and even those Hawaiian kinds of shirts...you know, the ones with palm trees and parrots and crap like that splattered all over. I don't know who buys them because one thing for sure no Quarter Rat would be caught dead in one. If nothing else, Quarter Rats have lots of self-respect, even the ones who don't make squat out on Jackson Square.

I forgot to tell you, there are a whole lot of other places Quarter Rats perform. Some are right there on Bourbon Street. Boy is that risky. If you get clobbered by someone coming out of a bar all lit up on hurricanes, there's not much left of you. Hurricanes are worse than anything, even absinthe. I'm sure a shrink could tell you what the difference is between hurricanes and absinthe. And there are even some Rats who perform on

Royal Street and over on Canal Street by where I work…a couple of jugglers, for example.

Well, I pick up a box of Milk Duds and take it to this guy, his name is Ernesto, who is sitting on this stool behind the counter reading a Batman comic book. He barely even looks at me, just says, "Buck twenty-five", and keeps reading. I dig out a buck twenty-five from my pocket and give it to him.

Then without looking up, he says, "Gonna be hot as hell today."

I agree. I look around. I'm thinking about maybe grabbing a Mr. Pibb to take home for later in the day. Maybe bring it with me to the hotel.

"They'll be in here today," Ernesto moans. He makes it sound like a bunch of little green men are on their way.

"Who will?" I ask.

"Oh, you know, the tourists." He's still reading Batman. "The people who get lost and end up over here from Bourbon Street."

Well, they *are* sort of like little green men, I think. Well, whole families of them, actually.

I'm figuring Ernesto must be pretty lonely today at the *Git n' Scram* because I've never heard him talk so much.

"Doesn't matter to me," he says as he flips a page of the comic book. "They always buy something."

"What about the pipe…the fancy one," I ask. "Ever sell one of those?"

"Which one?"

I point at the Sherlock Holmes."

"That? Nah."

I'm thinking maybe I could buy it and do a gig as Sherlock Holmes. It would probably be easy. I would just need to get one of those hats—kind of a tweed or plaid thing with a rim in the front and back and flaps that tie on top. And a cape sort of thing, too. Just walk around like you're real smart and thinking real hard like you're pretending to solve a mystery, and say crap like, "Elementary, my dear Watson…elementary."

I've never seen any of the Rats do that. It's good to store away ideas like this. Like I said, you can see how good I am at it, at coming up with great ideas. Working as a bellhop has really sharpened my sense of business, that's for sure.

"Saw Clifford a bit ago. You know him, don't you?" Ernesto says. "He just got back from the flea market. Had a couple of shirts and some kinda piano string."

"Huh?" I say. I think it was a guitar string, but I don't say so. But knowing Clifford he might try playing his guitar with a piano string. He's always getting junk mixed up.

"Says he'll be doing some stuff over at Jackson Square once he gets the routine worked out." Ernesto sets the comic book down and goes over and bangs the AC unit a couple of times. It seems to help. All of a sudden it's blowing hard as hell. There's a thermometer outside the window. He looks out and checks the temp. "Yep, just what I thought. Ninety-seven already."

Just then a bunch of people walk in—a family just like Ernesto predicted. He knows his stuff, all right.

They look around then put a whole load of candy bars on

the counter, and soda pop, and even T-shirts and a comic book. They pay for it and shovel it all into a bag they're carrying. Tourists are always carrying bags of some kind so they can cram all the stupid shit they buy into it. The woman hands the bag to the man and they all leave.

"See what I told you," Ernesto says. He picks up the comic book again. "Ever read one of these?"

I shake my head.

"Let me tell you, it's pretty involved."

I suspect it is. Some of those comics are real deep. I heard Spiderman is the most difficult of all. I suspect there are professors in English Lit departments all over the country who teach whole courses in Batman and Spiderman or whatever. Someone at The Chart Room mentioned it, if I remember correctly.

Ernesto tells me the plot of the story. Yikes, it is complicated all right and he's barely a third of the way into the comic, so you can see there's still a lot more to come.

I tell Ernesto that I might pick up one of the comics and read it when I don't have anything else to do. Right now I'm busy as hell with all the stuff I'm trying to do at once.

9

I go back to my place. The AC is cranking it out pretty well. I sit in a chair and prop my feet up and look out the window at the courtyard and eat the Milk Duds. I'm starting to get some energy back but the heat and all the Charlie Chaplin jumping around in the courtyard wore me out pretty bad, so I lay down.

I wake up in a panic thinking I might have overslept for work but it's only three o'clock and I don't need to be there until four. I sure wish I had a Mr. Pibb. That would get me going in no time what with all the sugar in it. But I'm not about to go down to the *Git 'n Scram* just to get one, so I get cleaned up instead.

I'm real good about that—about making sure I look tip-top at the hotel. See, people judge you in every possible way when you have an important position like I do. They look you over *real* close. Consider this, you're handling some pretty precious stuff in those bags—expensive suits, silk ties from Italy or Turkey or someplace like that. And the wigs the old ladies wear. Did you know some of those are made out of actual human hair, not horse hair, for example. And expensive perfume, too...like French perfume, I mean. Not the ratty crap you get at CVS or Target or Walmart. None of that shit.

Usually I shave, but not always because it's the fad nowadays to have this three-day old stubbly beard. One time this actor stayed at the hotel. He had a stubbly beard and you know he has tons of money and can buy all the razor blades he wants. See, I'm kind of a fashion god when it comes to stuff like that.

So, I get cleaned up and comb my hair. I'm lucky because I have most of my hair, not like a few of the Rats at The Chart Room whose hair is real thin, what they have of it. They pull it across their head in thin strips. And one even wears a toup. That's what's we used to call it back in Baltimore...a toup. My uncle has one because he's fairly bald so he wears this big thick toup. It doesn't fool anyone, mostly because it's way too bushy. Sorta like it's made out of racoon skin or maybe even horse hair...you know, the stuff from the tail. Something like that.

Anyway, I fluff my hair and make it look real good, which is kind of a waste when you consider I have to put on the stupid red cap.

I check the time: twenty minutes to four, just enough to get to the hotel and dress up. I put on the shoes I had fixed yesterday. Remember, the ones I took to the cobbler for new soles. I buzz across the Quarter until I get to Royal Street and then chug my way up to Canal Street. Lots of tourists out...everywhere.

I get to the hotel at exactly five minutes to four and change into my uniform and go to the front of the hotel just as Ollie is coming in from the day shift. He's a nice guy and he works real hard.

"Wow, busy as hell, Rubin," Ollie says. "Like almost when there's a convention or something."

You can tell it must have been a busy day because Ollie's cap is kinda perched on the side of his head as if he didn't have a minute to straighten it up. It can be a problem if the little rubber band thing gets too loose. That's something that management is not very good at in my opinion. Someday I might go to HR and tell them they need to fix the cap problem if they want to improve employee morale. Little stuff like that can make a big difference. I didn't tell you but I've been kinda watching to see if a job ever comes up in HR.

"Made good money today, though," he says. He taps his front pocket where he stuffed all the bills and heads into the hotel.

Well, it isn't ten seconds before an airport bus pulls up in front of the hotel and a slew of people tumble out. The bus driver unloads a mountain of bags onto the sidewalk.

"Hey boy, wanna grab that one for me?" this guy says.

"And this one, too," the woman with him says.

Well, I do more than just that. I've got this routine down and know exactly how to handle a pack of people like this. I get one of those carts hotels use and wheel it over and stack the bags sky high onto it.

"Careful, this one's got some pretty good stuff in it," one

of them says. He never says what it is.

I'm figuring it's got maybe a bunch of that French perfume like I talked about. Or maybe the silk ties. Crap like that.

You wouldn't believe how quickly I got the whole mess organized on the cart—I mean in practically no time at all. There's a real skill to it. It takes a lot of know-how to get everything put on just right.

I follow the people into the hotel and wait while they check in. This couple wants to have their picture taken with me. The guy says they're in N.O. for their anniversary, and says they came from Omaha, and he never saw anyone dressed like me so he wants a picture for the kids when they get back home.

I do it and even before I get his bags up to their room he jams a five-dollar bill into the top pocket of my coat. He tells me about all the restaurants they plan to hit while there here. And the bars too, just about every one of them up and down Bourbon street.

Let me tell you, this day is starting out like a bang, just like Ollie said. Boy am I glad I got my shoes fixed at the cobbler.

So I wait for everyone to check in and I end up having to pose for a couple more pictures. This one old lady says, "Billy is gonna *love* this, wait till he sees it."

I'm starting to feel like a movie star. Or like those people who wander around through the casinos in Vegas, the ones who look like the Rat Pack—you know, Dean Martin, and Frank Sinatra, and Sammy Davis Jr. And there were others too, but I can't remember who they were. I've never seen the fake ones because I've never been to Vegas but I heard there are lots of them, like they're all over the place in the casinos is what I heard. The trick is they let you take their picture for a couple of bucks. A friend of mine went to Vegas and got a picture while he was there. He showed it to me. I'll tell you, they didn't look like the real Rat Pack at all. They looked pretty phony in my opinion.

But he said everyone in the casino says, "Hey look, over there…there's the Rat Pack! Or, wow, look, it's Deano, and Frank Sinatra, and Sammy Davis Jr." Cripes, what people won't spend their money on. Just go piss it away at the roulette wheel is what I say.

But then I get this idea…see, I'm always thinking. What if I get a couple of other Quarter Rats and we do a Rat Pack gig in Jackson Square. We might be able to get plastic masks of them to put on and we could slink around through the Quarter for pictures like they do in Vegas. The Rat Pack always did that, they slinked around a lot. I guess it made them look cool or something. Anyway, maybe it would be better to go over to Bourbon Street or Royal Street. When people get enough hurricanes in them they don't see very straight so we wouldn't have to look perfect or anything like that. Just get these masks and do a lot of slinking and look real cool.

When I get back to the front of the hotel a horse and buggy pulls up. Eddie Clabberman is driving it. Remember Eddie from The Chart Room, he's the Rat who's writing the tome that never gets finished.

"Hey Rubin," he calls. "They sent me over here to get some people. The Johnsons, they said. That's all I know. Can you see if they're inside?"

I go in and head straight to the bar. You know right away that's where they'll be. I call out, "John-son family…your-*buggy*-is-waiting." I makes it sound very formal, like it's the buggy for the Queen of England. People like it when I do that. It makes them feel real special.

They're sitting at the bar talking to Remy. I can tell they don't understand much of what he's saying. He's rambling on like crazy while he's mixing drinks. Me, I can understand him perfect, now that I am almost fluent in Cajun. I could do some interpreting, but Eddie has gotta get hoppin' real fast.

The man says, "Oh wow, that's for us. C'mon, let's go."

They get off the bar stools and follow me out—five of them in all. A man, a woman, two kids, and a granny-looking sorta person. I hope she doesn't get whiplash if the horse takes off all of a sudden. But I doubt that'll happen. Eddie knows his stuff when it comes to driving buggies. He knows how to talk to the horse to get it to do what he wants.

They all get in the buggy. I have to help granny up. She needs to be strapped in, I'm thinking, but I don't see any seat belts. One sharp turn and granny is on the flagstone, and then they'd have to peel all that goo and crap from the street off her dress.

Eddie gives the reins a jiggle and the horse goes clomping down the street. I can hear him telling the people all the neat things they'll see. The buggy company teaches the drivers what to say on the tour. I've seen Eddie do it when I run into him as I cross the Quarter. He stops the buggy and says, "And over here on the left…" And then he points to a house where a famous person once lived. And everyone in the buggy leans over and says, "Wooow!" And then Eddie says something about the famous person who lived there.

He likes doing it especially when he's talking about a writer. Eddie once told me about all the writers who used to live in the Quarter, it's a pretty long list. He said some of them were real poor and barely had a nickel, like almost as poor as a lot of the Rats who live here now. They probably didn't eat Campbell's Pork & Beans from the can like Jim Yute does. They probably weren't that poor.

I don't remember who all of the writers were but I think one was that Faulkner guy, and another one was that Tennessee Williams fella. There are signs stuck on the wall in front of the houses they used to live in.

I never could figure out why Tennessee Williams called himself Tennessee if he lived in the Quarter. Probably because it wouldn't be so cool to call yourself New Orleans Williams, or Louisiana Williams, or French Quarter Williams. That's what I'm figuring. Doesn't sound so great.

Eddie says it's the heat in N.O. that makes you write good stuff. Like it moves your brain cells around differently and you can come up with great ideas.

That's something I might study when I'm a shrink. I could see if people in Alaska write as good as people in N.O. It will probably become a famous study that all the other shrinks talk about the way they do with the junk that real famous shrink came up with. What was his name? Oh yeah, Sigmund Freud, I think that was it.

Did you ever see a picture of Freud? He always looks grumpy as hell. I don't know, maybe that's how you get when people come to you and are always carping about something or other all the time. And he's always smoking a cigar in the pictures, which maybe screwed up his stomach and makes him feel like he's about to barf—especially if it's a Cuban cigar. Those babies are strong. I sucked on one of them once when I was sitting in front of The Chart Room—geez, I felt like I was gonna keel over right there.

Anyway, there certainly have been a lot of writers in the Quarter in the old days. I don't know if any of them wrote tomes, but Eddie would know all about it. I'll ask him next time I see him in The Chart Room.

10

Boy, let me tell you, I'm flying for three hours straight. I can't figure out what's going on. I don't think it's people in for a convention, but you never know because they have at least one going on almost all the time in N.O.

In fact, the last convention just ended. It was a bunch of docs who specialize in kidneys. They're called urologists is what I heard. They have this real stupid sense of humor. You'd sure as hell need one to specialize in kidneys, I think. Well anyway, Remy told me that a couple of them were sitting at the bar and one said, "Is this a piss-poor convention, or what?" And the other kidney docs roared like hell. I don't know, I guess it's a typical kidney-doc joke or something.

So, it could be that there's a convention of some type and I don't know it. Usually, the hotel tells us so we're ready for the flood of people. But even if they say nothing, you can tell because about five o'clock in the afternoon you get a jillion people coming back to the hotel wearing those paper stickers with their name on it. Some of them even go to dinner with it on. It's probably not a bad idea because once you start knocking back hurricanes you forget who you are real quick.

It's almost non-stop people all afternoon. I have to fill up my gigantic cup with iced-tea at least four times. The hotel lets me do it for free. I take it to the restaurant and they top it off and then I set it on a small table just inside the door of the hotel.

At eight o'clock I get my dinner break. I usually go down Canal Street to a place called Napoleon's that has a small bar and a few tables. Don't ask me why they call it Napoleon's. I doubt he ever ate there.

Actually, there are a couple of places in the Quarter called Napoleon's. Probably the most famous one is over on Royal Street. It's a snazzy place and real pricey and it's always filled with tons of people. I prefer the hole-in-the-wall joint on Canal Street. Practically every time I go there I get red beans and rice. Everyone in N.O. eats red beans and rice on Monday...it's sort of a tradition thing, I guess. But most restaurants serve it the rest of the week, too.

I never had red beans and rice until I came to N.O. Somehow eating rice slopped with beans didn't sound so great, but then one afternoon I had it at The Chart Room with Sab. He's sort of an expert when it comes to food. He knows everything about food. He could probably be a chef if he wasn't working for Popeye.

So, I had the red beans and rice with Sab. Yikes, it was unbelievable. And they usually put some Cajun sausage in...Remy told me it's called andouille.

Some of the restaurants serve red beans and rice along with a piece of fried chicken—southern-fried chicken that's real crispy. You can get the whole meal for almost nothing. Quarter Rats eat more red beans and rice than probably anyone on the planet.

Well, now I'm kinda addicted to the stuff. I eat a plate of it almost every evening at Napoleon's. I'm not sure who invented it…the red beans and rice, I mean. I'm wondering if it might have been Napoleon himself. That's probably why they always made paintings of him with his hand stuck in his shirt. He was probably trying to hold his belly in so he didn't look fat or whatever. The crazy thing is, red beans and rice doesn't make you fat because it's full of protein, loaded with energy. Most days I'm pretty worn out by the time I get on my dinner break and then after a plate of red beans and rice I'm charged up and ready to go again. Of course, having a big Mr. Pibb might have something to do with it.

It feels good to be sitting in Napoleon's. It's always nice and cool in there. One thing you can say, their AC unit works well even though the restaurant is sort of crappy inside. And they have ceiling fans that barely turn at all, but they push the cool air from the AC around good enough. That's what makes it a nice place. Sometimes a tourist or a whole pile of them or even some convention people will stick their head in the front door and turn around and leave pretty quick like everyone in the place has smallpox or something. Boy, if they only knew they they're missing out on the best red beans and rice in practically all of N.O.

A lot of times I run into other Rats there. It's a real popular place for them. I've been going in so long I know most of the people who work there…well, there are only about two or three, but I know them by name.

Elsie, the waitress, mostly works the evenings. She always talks to me for a while. One time I wore my cap when I came in. I usually take it off but I forgot to. Elsie thought it was super cool. I told her they give you one when you work at the hotel, along with the jacket and the black pants. We have to buy our own white shirt and a black bowtie. I forgot to tell you that, we wear a black bowtie—it's part of the whole rigamarole, the costume. I managed to get a real cheap bowtie at the flea market. Cool thing about it is that it's one of those clip-on jobs so I don't have to mess with tying it. Which is good because I'd probably end up strangling myself if I tried to. So at the end of my shift I just stuff the dumb thing in the pocket of my jacket. I don't dare take it home. You wouldn't believe how easy it is to lose junk even in a place as small as mine, what with all the crud I have jammed in it.

Elsie sets down this big platter of red beans and rice. I mix the beans and the rice together with my fork. That's the trick. You need to get it perfectly mixed.

"Busy at the hotel?" Elsie asks.

"You can't believe," I say.

"A convention or something maybe, huh?"

"Yeah, maybe."

"Nutha Pibb?"

"That would be great!" I hand her my glass. They give you

free refills at Napoleon's.

Elsie heads off to get the drink; I dive into the beans and rice. Even after a couple of spoonfuls I can feel the energy come pouring back into me. Almost like Popeye—the real Popeye not the guy Sab works for—when he inhales the spinach.

Just then, three fellas come into Napoleon's. They don't look like they're locals and they don't look like they're at a convention and, besides, they all got cowboy hats on. You do see some people in the Quarter wearing cowboy hats now and then, but they're usually from Texas or Colorado or wherever.

One of them says, "Well now, check out this chuck wagon, will ya?"

I'm having some trouble understanding them because I don't speak all that much cowboy. Not that it matters since I'm just eating my red beans and rice and minding my business, but I'm wondering what if they come to the hotel? See, with what I do, you gotta be ready for everything.

"Whatcha say, want some grub?" one of the other ones says.

They sit at the bar and order beer. Pretty soon they're talking to the bartender and everyone is laughing like hell. I never saw anything like it. I don't know what they're talking about but even Elsie is roaring like crazy. I guess they have lots of good jokes out in Texas and Colorado.

I check my watch. Yikes, time to go. I pay Elsie and I'm out the door and down the street.

Well, when I get back to the hotel I find out that three

cowboys checked in. They left their bags in the lobby and went out for some "grub", the desk clerk says.

I got a pretty good idea who she's talking about.

A couple of taxis pull up and unload, and then Eddie Clabberman brings his horse and buggy up to the curb in front of the hotel. He talks to the horse real smooth, saying stuff like, "Whoa, fella…whoa."

They've been gone a couple of hours, I'm figuring he gave them the first-class tour. Probably hit all the writer's houses.

Everyone seems to have made it through okay, though granny is looking a little blasted…almost as if she took a tumble off the buggy like I said might happen.

I help her down. Cripes, she's all twisted around like a Frito or something. The others get off and grab her arms and try to untwist her. I think it's still possible she got a little whiplash. Even with a buggy driver like Eddie the horses sometimes jolt forward. Let me tell you, that would not be good for granny with her neck that's about as skinny as a bread stick. But little by little, they're getting her straightened out…more or less.

Pretty soon the cowboys come rolling down the street. They're still laughing to beat hell. Probably had lots of beer. When they get to me they stop and stare like they recognize me, but I can tell they're not too sure because I didn't have my cap on in Napoleon's. I try not to wear it even if I go over to the drugstore to get a Snickers or some Milk Duds. First of all, I don't want some store clerk thinking I'm about to hold him up and am wearing a silly costume to get him distracted and not look at my face. That's the kind of thing crooks sometimes do so you don't remember who they are.

So one of the cowboys looks at me and says, "*Wow!* Now *that's* what I call a hat! Geez! But I guess yer the guy who handles the saddle bags, huh? Well, we got a couple of 'em sittin' inside, if'n yer can give 'em a grab."

Now I got this figured out pretty good. If Sab was here, he could talk to them real easy, what with all the languages he speaks.

I follow them in and put their saddle bags on a cart. We go to the elevator and ride it up to the eleventh floor where their room is.

One of the cowboys is wearing a real flashy belt with this huge buckle that's practically the size of a manhole cover. It's got a picture of a guy riding a horse that's jumping all around. I don't know why you'd want to ride a horse that's going crazy like that, but cowboys seem to like to.

He says, "So where's the best place to go on Bourbon Street to get some good hooch? Reckon they's lots a places, huh. Dun matter. Heck, we'll jes hit 'em all, prob-ly."

It turns out they're not from Texas or Colorado, they're from Wyoming and they're in N.O. on business, though they don't say what kinda business. I can tell you this, those saddle bags weigh a ton, and I mean a ton, so I'm figuring they're filled with something like super-heavy belt buckles kinda like the one the guy has on. They probably got plans to peddle them in some of the stores in the Quarter, but it might be just an excuse to come down here and go to Bourbon Street and drink a bunch of hooch. You'd think they probably have hooch up in Wyoming, but I doubt that they have anything like Bourbon Street. And anyway, how many belt buckles can you sell in Wyoming if everybody already has one.

There are lots of little stores in the Quarter that sell trinkets and crap. I mean you can sell anything under the sun and the tourists will snatch it up like crazy. Like candles that are in tall colored glass jars. The candles are all scented with perfume and junk and there's always some kind of picture of N.O. on the outside. That's the kinda crap I'm talking about.

Boy are the cowboys ever generous. When we get to the room, they each drop a five spot on me. The one guy who asked about my cap keeps looking at it. I suspect they don't have anything like it in Wyoming...that's what I'm guessing. For that matter, I don't think you could wear one while riding a horse because the little rubber band thing would snap pretty quick. Especially if it was one of those super-hyper horses like on his belt buckle.

When I get down to the front of the hotel there's a whole string of people waiting to get their bags inside. I can't figure out what's the deal with all these people. They don't look like they're going to a convention or anything. One of the men says, "Ah hi, Mr. Rubin, could you please bring these inside."

Oh, I forgot to tell you, I have this brass name-plate sort of thing on my coat that says RUBIN on it. It's something that HR pushes real hard. At least I think it was an HR idea but I'm not totally sure because I don't know everything HR does to make our jobs seem better. Got news for HR. You want to make my job better? Scrap the monkey hat. That's a good place to start.

Anyway, I have this name plate on my coat and because my name being Rubin no one knows if it's my first name or my last name. You can tell most of the time when they're not sure, they just say, "Hey pal," or "Hey buddy." Stuff like that. You can see, HR doesn't have all the answers. I'll get this straightened out when I get a job in HR as soon as a position comes open. I bet positions turn over real fast when you consider that you could run out of HR ideas pretty quick. But me, I have so many ideas stored up I could work in HR for years and years and not run out. Like in my case, HR could have a name plate made that says something like RUBIN (FIRST NAME). See how easy it would be. When you work out in front of the hotel like I do, pretty soon you know all the ins and outs of how the joint operates and what would make it better.

For example, if people come out of the hotel and they're all ticked off it's probably because the ice machine on the floor got jammed or the candy machine is empty, crud like that. It can make you pissed as hell. When you see people super grumpy you know something is really bugging them. It's another reason why I'll be a great shrink…all those tricks they have about knowing what's going on inside a person's head even when they don't tell you. It's almost like they have a kind of radar system that can read brain waves. I'm pretty good at it already, so when I'm finally a shrink I'll be even better.

This is one of the busiest days since I started working at

the hotel and I still can't figure it out. And hot…*wow!* I went through about four giant mugs of iced tea.

Before I know it, my shift is over. I go inside and take off my red coat and hat and put them in the room behind the reception desk.

On my way out, Claudia says, "How'd it go today, Rubin?" Claudia is a real nice Quarter Rat, though I almost hate to call her a Rat because she's so sweet. She works at the reception desk.

"Best day of all…maybe ever," I tell her.

She gives me this nice smile and a wink.

The Quarter is real quiet as I head down Royal Street. Funny, I mean there were so many people coming into the hotel and now it's almost abandoned. Just as good. I've had my fill for one day of grannies and cowboys and tons of bags.

As I get to Ramona's place, I see her standing on the balcony. I call up to her.

"Hey Rubin," she says, "how are you doing? Wanna come up?"

Boy, do I ever.

Ramona's place is cool…it smells like mangos. She must have just come out of the shower. Her hair is combed down and sort of wet. She usually works until two a.m. or so, but she tells me she got off early. Not too much going on. Three cowboys who told really great jokes came in. Now, I'm wondering how they escaped from the hotel without me seeing them. I figure they probably know all the tricks…remember how cowboys were always sneaking out of jail in the old movies, the westerns? Oh well, doesn't matter.

Ramona pulls a couple of cold beers from the refrigerator. I ask if I can use her shower to get the grime off me. I always feel grimy after I work, like I rolled around on the flagstone in Jackson Square or something.

I come out feeling tons better. We sit and have a couple of beers and then goof off all night long.

11

In the morning I head home. I feel great even though I didn't get a whole lot of sleep. In fact, I feel so great I do a little of my Charlie Chaplin routine in the courtyard for about fifteen minutes. That's the whole thing, being young as I am I have plenty of energy to work on the Chaplin duck walk even with just a little bit of sleep.

It goes pretty well. I'm getting the routine down without much trouble, even the stupid thing where he flicks his leg up behind him when he walks down the street. All in all I don't spend much time on the routine because I'm hungry as hell. In fact, I'm so hungry I could probably eat a whole sausage PoBoy from Buster's. But I don't go to Buster's. I change into jeans and go over to the café.

When I go into the courtyard out back of the café, first thing I do is look around just to make sure the morning won't be trashed by lots of people I don't want to talk to. But sure enough, Clifford Ritter's there eating his beignets and licking the sugar off his fingers. I sit at the table. It isn't long before he says, "So, wanna hear something crazy, Rubin?"

Here we go. Get ready but don't expect much because Clifford never ever tells me anything crazy. But I nod anyway. The problem is if you don't answer, he asks again like he thinks you might be deaf or something. It really pisses me off.

"Believe it or not, there actually was a guitar string at the flea market…the one I went to yesterday."

"Oh," I say. Not so crazy really, I think.

"So, I got it and it cost almost nothing, like around fifty cents. And I got a couple of faded shirts, too. I'm not sure, but the guitar string looks a lot like a piano string. But I think it'll work anyway."

"Have you tried it?" I ask.

"Tried what?"

Earth to Clifford. Earth to Clifford. "The string. The piano string."

Franka brings my quiche and coffee.

Clifford doesn't answer. He tears apart a beignet and manages to get most of it into his mouth all at once. "Good idea," he sputters, "I'll do it when I get home." He dusts his hands on his pants and swills in a big gulp of his latte.

"Here's another one," he says.

"Another what?"

"Another crazy thing."

"Oh."

"All night long when I was driving the hack I just kept going from one bar to the next."

"Okay."

"Now, that's real crazy. You see I usually end up going all

over N.O…Uptown, the Garden District, lots of hotels…junk like that."

"Okay."

"But not last night. I just went from one bar to the next in the French Quarter."

"Okay."

"And guess what?"

"You win."

"I had these three cowboys."

"Really."

He shakes the sugar off his hand and holds up three fingers to make his point. Of course, all kinds of sugar is still on his fingertips. "That's right…three," he says.

"Hmm."

"Yeah, they were pretty well gone. Lotsa hooch…that's what they called it. So anyway, I only took them about a block or two, like from Bourbon Street to some joint on Royal and then to a couple places on Rampart and Bienville and to a place back on Burgundy. I mean, they hit them all. They said they were from Wyoming and that they're here to sell a bunch of belt buckles, if you can imagine that."

See what I told you. I have real good radar like shrinks have. Remember, I was pretty certain the saddle bags were full of belt buckles, or at least one of them was.

We pretty much beat this topic to death, I'm thinking, so I ask Clifford if he has a guitar case for when he does his gig in the Quarter. But before he answers, he gets up to show me his Mr. Bojangles routine. I push back pretty far from the table just in case.

He starts singing a little, you know, the part that says, *He jumped so high. He jumped so high. And then he'd lightly touch down.*

Next thing I know, he's about three feet off the ground. I mean *waaay* up there. He clicks his heels together and lands on the ground. On both feet! Pretty miraculous!

"See, I worked on it most of the day when I got back from the flea market," he says.

"Not bad. But you still need a guitar case." I explain that all the Rats who play music in the Quarter use them for tips.

Clifford thinks about this for a while. You can tell he hasn't given it much thought. Not very good at thinking fast, like thinking on your feet is what I mean. It's the big difference between being a hack and doing what I do—having to know exactly which bag to grab first and how to stack them all on the cart that I roll into the hotel. There's a real art to it. Some of the other Rats who work at the hotel never quite figure it out, not as well as I do anyway.

Clifford says, "Might need to make another trip over to Algiers and pick one up, I guess. Sort of hate to get back on that old ferry again and ride it across that shark-infested river. Not my favorite thing. Might try the flea market first…might."

I tell Clifford about my idea to do a Rat Pack thing in the Quarter. He thinks it's a good idea. He tells me there's a shop over on Poydras Street that sells all kind of costumes. He says they probably even have Rat Pack face masks. I know where Poydras Street is because I get a lot of questions about it. Like one time these people said they wanted to go to Tchoupitoulas and Poydras. Problem was it came out sounding like Chopapoodle's ass and Toydoll Streets. Don't know how the hell they got that. Well, from my experience hearing it all the time, I knew exactly what they meant.

Well, there we are talking about the Rat Pack thing when you're not gonna believe what happens. Horace Slagg comes bowling into the café. Remember him, Horace, the dude who is always trying to hit on Sab's action? He looks around and sees me and races up to the table.

"Hey pal, seen Sab?" he says.

"Not my day to watch him," I say, just like last time he asked that stupid question.

It always pisses Horace off when I say that. He gives a shitty little smile and grunts. Not like Popeye—Popeye mumbles. Horace grunts. Especially when he talks to us dweebs. I never hear him grunt when he talks to Sab. It's a dweeb thing and it's annoying as hell—but not nearly as much as the fact that he's even here talking to me.

I take a sip of coffee. "He's out of town with Joey," I finally tell him. "Don't know when he's coming back."

Horace grunts again and turns and starts tacking his way out but then stops and says, "You going over to Sab's place sometime?"

"Why?" I say.

"Heard you gotta pick up his mail."

"Need to get your hearing checked, Horace."

"It's true, isn't it?"

"Maybe."

"Great, I'll come with you."

"I don't know when I'm going."

"We can go when we're done here." Horace pulls up a chair and sits at the table and waves to Franka for a cup of coffee.

"Why do you want to go to Sab's?" I say.

"I got this photo I need to give him. He's gonna love it." Horace taps a briefcase that he's carrying. I didn't notice it when he came in. How would I? Who would notice it, right? The ridiculous shirts he wears is distraction enough. Did I tell you about them? He wears these shirts called Mexican Wedding Shirts. I know a Rat who sometimes peddles them in the Quarter—he told me what they are. He sets up a cart and sells them right on the street. That's the thing about the Quarter, you can push just about anything. Okay, I admit I did buy one of them once, but I never wore it. Anyway, Horace likes to wear them, and he usually wears a gold chain around his neck, too. A pretty heavy-looking chain. But his face is always as pale as can be. About the color of his Wedding Shirt. The guy is a vampire incognito. Now there's a word for you—incognito. Eddie the tome writer used it once. I looked it up and now I use it all the time.

"I might not go to Sab's till this afternoon," I tell Horace. "I forgot…I'm…uh…I've got to run an errand."

"Yeah, Rubin's probably going over to Algiers with me," Clifford says.

I have no idea where he came up with that, but he sure bailed my ass out of marching around the Quarter with

Horace. Think how fun that would be!

"Why the hell would you go to Algiers," Horace says. "Nothing over there, that's for sure."

That's another thing about Horace, he's always telling everyone what to do. At the hotel, like I *never* do that. When HR trained us, they gave us lots of instructions about it. Let me tell you, there are loads of places I'd like to tell people not to go to in the quarter. But I don't. HR said just give them directions and let them worry about the rest. Like, for example, don't tell them granny could fall off the horse cart, or get whiplash, or get crunched up into a knot after a hot two-hour ride.

"Huh, too bad," Horace says. "About not going over to Sab's I mean. I know he'd really like to see the photo."

I explain to Horace that I don't think Sab will be able to see it until he gets back from Mississippi, so what's the point.

Horace says nothing. He just grunts. You can tell he's pissed—having to sit with a couple of dweebs doesn't help.

Anyway, I know exactly why Horace wants to go to Sab's. Simple, he really just wants to check out all the hot pictures Sab has pinned to his walls. I'm sure of it.

"I could go over to Algiers with you," Horace says.

"Why am I getting a bad feeling about this?" I say.

"Ha, ha, ha…funny, funny."

"Thought you hate Algiers."

Horace doesn't answer. "How about we go to Sab's first. In case he comes back early."

Just then Popeye comes into the café. Horace sees him

and goes over to the table. They know each other, I guess, both being photographers.

I hear Horace say, "Hey pal, how's it going? How's everything at The Poteet?"

Sab once told me that Horace comes into Mike's photo studio now and then. He calls it The Poteet. Popeye doesn't seem so happy to see Horace. I hear him mumble something, something about "Naw-lins."

Horace has his back to me so I'm thinking it's a good time to sneak out while he's not looking. But just then, Horace turns and says, "Can't go with you guys to Algiers."

...disappointment!

"Just remembered something I need to do." He shakes Popeye's hand and streams out of the café.

12

So, I go to St. Anne Street and get Sab's mail and put it in his apartment. I have no plans to join Clifford on his trip to Algiers, I mean the ferry probably will turn over, what with all Clifford's bad karma. I'm not worried about river sharks. I know there aren't any, but if the boat did turn over, I'd be afraid of swallowing big gulps of muddy river water and then I'd probably have to get my stomach pumped out over at Doc Mellman's. There's no telling what kind of crud is in the river. I mean, think about it, all the stuff that floats down from way up north wherever the river starts. I'm not sure exactly where that is...Iowa, maybe, or maybe Canada. Someplace like that. I heard nobody really knows where the Mississippi starts. It's kind of like a long time ago when they were looking for the beginning of the Nile River.

I've got some time to kill so I figure I'll go and see about the Rat Pack masks at the shop on Poydras Street, the one Clifford told me about. I head down Peters Street and cross Canal Street and continue on down Tchoupitoulas until I get to Poydras. Sure enough, there it is just like Clifford said. One thing about Clifford, he may not be the best *Bojangles* jumper in the world but when it comes to streets in the quarter, he knows his shit.

I go in the shop. It's got this picture painted on the window of one of those jesters you see all around during Mardi Gras. That real doofus-sort of face of some dork wearing a silly green and yellow and purple hat that jesters wear with the three flaps and little round balls hanging off the end of each.

Oh, I forgot to tell you, remember when we were talking about the mimes? The ones that don't move…you know, the one's that barely even breath? Well, there used to be this Rat over in Jackson Square who was dressed like a Mardi Gras jester. He'd stand in front of St. Louis Cathedral for hours. You'd think because he was supposed to be a jester and all that he'd want to hop around and do jester kinda shit. I'm not sure what that is but there must be a stupid jester routine of some kind. Anyway, he didn't have much of a routine. I guess that's why he did the mime thing where you don't move a muscle. He never made much money. He actually had two routines. The second one was the dumb old trick of being stuck in an invisible box. That's the problem with a lot of the Rats, they need to get more imaginative. You've gotta push your brain cells real hard if you're gonna come up with something great to do. Anyway, when he was stuck in the box he pretended to be real confused like he was dumb as shit and couldn't figure out how he got in or how to get out. And it was sorta convincing because you know jesters are dumb as hell or else they wouldn't be jesters.

So, the store has a big picture of a jester painted on the window, and it is says: Mardi Gras Costumes and Masks — Beads and Party Treats.

I go inside. Boy, is it ever dusty smelling. Like all the costumes need a good flea dip or something. And let me tell you, there are loads of costumes in the place. I mean racks and racks and racks of them. You're probably wondering how the place can stay in business if Mardi Gras happens only once a year. Easy, because people in N.O. love to party.

I'm digging through the costumes when this person comes up and says, "Mo-nin…can I hep ya? Lookin' fer enna thin special? If ya are…we prob-ly got it."

I tell her about the Rat Pack thing and that all I really need is a few masks.

"Whew! Now that's a tall orda. But might have some."

She goes over to a table that's stacked with masks. I never saw so many in my life. There was even a Richard Nixon mask. And it looks pretty real, too. Long kinda square nose. I put it on and go over to the mirror and put my hands up and shake my head and say, "I am not a crook!"

"You do that real well," she says. "That there's one of our best-sellin' masks. The other one people like is this one." She hands me a Bill Clinton mask.

I put it on and, in that throaty voice of his, say, "I-yuh did not have sex with thaaeet woman."

Now the salesperson is really laughing.

"Why, heck, yer perty good at that. You should be on TV or somethin'."

I never told you that when I was in Baltimore, I really did think about being an actor or one of those stand-up comedy guys maybe, something like that because I can do great impressions. I might even do them sometimes when I'm a shrink. If you can get people laughing they won't be so bummed over all the bad crap that's going on in their life, that's how I look at it. Anyway, you won't believe all the people I can do an impression of. It's a real big list, almost everyone you can think of. I do a great George Bush, you know the second Bush prez. I saw an interview with him after he was no longer president. The interviewer asked him what he's doing now. He says, "Got me some pages on the inner-*netsh.*" Not sure what he meant. Facebook, maybe. Who knows? He's easy to do, though.

I do impressions of lots of politicians. They're a snap because they are all real goons. When they give their speeches in Washington, like some Senator or whatever, they always pretend they're talking to loads of other politicians. But actually, most of the time there is no one else in the room. I saw this once when I accidently turned on C-SPAN in the middle of the day. Well, you see, this politician is talking, and he's real dramatic, and his arms are swinging all over the place like an octopus or something, and he's pounding on the table in front of him…and he's practically crying he's so worked up. And then the camera shows the room and it's totally empty. I mean not a freakin' soul in the entire place. Everyone's out playing golf. I bet that's what's going on. It's one of the best jobs in the world. Probably even better than being a Professor of English Lit, most likely.

"Holy guacamole!" the person at the store blurts. "Look at this, will ya? And I was ready to give up." She holds up a mask that looks a lot like Deano. At least I think it does. I'm not totally sure how he looked—he was pretty much before my time.

So I pay her for the mask. Five dollars, not too bad. I'll come back some other time and see if they have one of Frank Sinatra and Sammy Davis Jr. For now, I'll just see what I can do with this one.

I put it on and go outside. It's a good time to give it a try on my way back to the Quarter. I kinda do this real slinky walk down the street the way the Rat Pack always did. I pass probably six or seven people or so. They all stop and stare at me.

"Hey, where ya going, Deano?" someone yells, laughing.

I don't answer because Deano probably wouldn't answer a dumb-ass question like that. I just slink past. It's clear that the mask is working. I knew it would. I had this pretty well figured out from the start. Once I get an idea in my head and things start clicking there's no stopping me. So, you can see how easy it will be for me to work in HR when a position comes open.

I figure before I get to Jackson Square I better take the mask off so people don't start throwing money at me or something. It might not be a bad idea, though. But I figure I better wait until we get the entire routine worked out with the other Rats. And we'll have to practice what we're gonna do.

That's gonna be pretty hard because Rats never stick to anything for very long. I know all about how important practice is. Look how long I've gone over my Charlie Chaplin routine—three times already, probably. And by the time I'm ready to do it, you'll think I really am Charlie Chaplin. I even tried working on the routine at the hotel once when I wasn't so busy. I had to be real careful to make sure no one was looking. You know, dressed up like an organ grinder monkey and doing a Charlie Chaplin walk and all.

You really have to concentrate when you're doing these impressions. I'm kinda worried I might not be able to find Rats who can concentrate as hard as I do when we finally do the Rat Pack gig in Jackson Square or wherever.

But when you think about it, the Rat Pack never looked like they were concentrating too much while they slinked through the casinos in Vegas. I'm talking about the *real* Rat Pack not the phony ones that are there now. The real ones had been doing it for so long—slinking around and all—that they could do it without even trying. They probably even slinked around the house when they were tiny little babies.

See, here's what you do. You walk like you're barely moving your feet. And you kinda swing your shoulders a little bit but not too much. And you gotta keep your elbows real close to your side, and your wrists sorta loose and dangly. There's a whole lotta crap you need to do to get it right. I think that's where the phony Rat Pack people get it all wrong. They kinda just bob up and down, that's sorta what I heard. Who's gonna believe that shit? I mean, come on.

Well, I'm walking along when coming right at me is Clifford Ritter. "Hey, cool!" he says. "Is that you, Rubin?"

"No, it's Deano, you dumb ass."

"The mask looks great. And I like the walk and all."

"I'm slinking. That's what the Rat Pack did when they walked around."

"Okay…I get it."

I take off the mask.

Clifford tries slinking around.

"Not too bad," I say.

"Yeah, I could probably be one of the guys. Anyway, I'm going over to Algiers to get a guitar case for my gig."

"What's that?" I say, pointing to a white plastic thing he's carrying.

"This? Oh, it's a life preserver. I don't trust the ones on the ferry. They look like they're all cracked and about to fall apart. This is one that you blow up. See, here's the tube you blow into. Kinda like what you do on an airplane that's about to crash into the ocean or something."

I shake my head. "Can you blow that thing up if you're in the river?"

"Well, yeah…probably. And I also got some anti-shark spray, just in case. I bought some a long time ago but never brought it with me till now." He shows it to me.

"It says it's for keeping bears away, Clifford."

"I know. But I'm sure it works fine for sharks, too. Anyhow, one of these days a ferry is gonna flip over, just wait. And then the river is gonna be filled with blood from all the shark attacks on the people. Well, not me. I'm ready."

"Have you ever seen a shark in the river. When you're going over to Algiers, I mean."

"You can't see them. The river is too muddy. Wanna come with me?"

I hand the bear spray back to Clifford. "Well, if nothing else, you won't have to worry about getting eaten by a bear in the river," I say. "No, I can't go. Anyway, I don't have a life preserver." You know, of course, Clifford is totally screwed up about this shark thing. All of a sudden it hits me, when I'm a shrink I'll probably know tons of junk about hypnosis. I'm sure they teach you all about that. I could give Clifford a couple of treatments and cure him pretty quick, I bet. From what I see, it sure would get rid of his fear of river sharks.

"If I ever see another life preserver, like maybe at a flea market or wherever, I'll pick one up for you," Clifford says. He starts heading to the ferry dock.

I look at my watch. I have this real expensive Timex that I always wear. I needed to get one for work at the hotel. People are always saying, "I'll be back for this in twenty minutes." And then they leave their bags with you. You never know, it could be full of real expensive stuff. Like silk ties, or what about those belt buckles the cowboys are planning to peddle. It's a lot of responsibility to make sure no one tries to lift one of the bags when you're not looking. So, I always check my watch to make sure I'm there when they return to get their bags.

Well anyway, I've got a lot of time until I need to go to work, so I'm thinking maybe it's not such a bad idea to go with

Clifford over to Algiers. If he's going to the music store, I could check the price of an instrument, a used one if they have cheap ones. Something I might be able to play in Jackson Square. I can't play any instruments but one thing I could do is get something that's real easy to play. Something like a tuba, for example. You probably only play about three notes on a tuba, being as big as it is and all. I could figure out how to play some tuba songs. Maybe even hook up with Clifford when he's doing the *Bojangles* thing and give a big blast from the tuba when he lands on his feet (hopefully) after leaping way up in the air. Something like that.

"Hey Clifford, wait up," I say. "I'll come with you." I fold the mask and stick it in my pocket. It's actually sorta cloth-like so it folds pretty easy.

"Cool!" Clifford says. "And if we have to, we can both hang onto the life preserver I brought."

I'm feeling safer already, what with the life preserver and the bear spray he has.

13

We get to the ferry dock down on the end of Canal Street. Clifford is checking out the boats. There's only one in service. It's coming across the river. He goes over to the edge of the dock and stares into the water.

"Looks pretty safe to me," he says. "Don't see anything stirring around down there. That would be a bad sign. I read about it once...I think it was in *National Geographic*. When they get about to attack, the sharks, they get all hopped up. Totally filled with adrenalin or something."

"You don't think they'd be over this close to the edge of the river, do you?" I might as well just go along with him.

"Oh sure. Sharks can flatten themselves out or whatever they need to do. But I don't see much going on."

The ferry pulls closer. You can tell the captain knows his shit because he's got it moving around one mile an hour or so. And they got a couple of guys up front to fling a rope over a big pole. They lower down a ramp and the cars drive off.

"This is where it gets risky," Clifford says. "You gotta make sure you don't unload one side more than the other and the boat starts leaning sideways and the next thing you know the whole thing is in the river."

I don't know where Clifford is from, before he came to the Quarter is what I mean, but it must've been some place where they grow a lot of corn or wheat because he doesn't know shinola about water or boats—not like me, being from Baltimore. I'm starting to think maybe it was a bad idea going over to Algiers with him.

Once the cars are loaded, the ferry chugs out of the dock. It has quite a few cars and quite a few people. The cat who's up on top of the boat steering it blows the foghorn about every twenty seconds or so. I'm not sure who he thinks is gonna miss seeing something as big as a river ferry out in the water, but he's probably just bored as hell and needs something to do.

All of a sudden Clifford roars, "There! Look, Rubin! *A shark!*"

"Where…I don't see one," I say.

"*There, there, there!*"

"That thing?"

"Yeah, yeah, it's a shark, like I said."

I grab the railing and look down. "It's a damn log, Clifford."

"A log?"

"Yes, a log. Do you see it swimming or anything?"

"Well…no, but…."

"But nothing. It's a log, Clifford. Okay? A log. The river's full of them."

Clifford takes the bear spray from his pants pocket and

sticks it in his shirt pocket. Just in case, probably.

We get across the river without tipping over. Clifford knows exactly where the music store is having been there before, and from his sense of direction as a hack. We walk for about five blocks or so. It's already pretty hot and it's not even noon yet.

The store's not very impressive, actually. Sorta wedged in between a dinky little Cajun restaurant and a barber shop. They've got a bunch of instruments in the window, but the window has bars on it so you can't break the glass and tear off with something important, I suppose. Anyhow, when you come right down to it most of the stuff looks pretty beat up.

We go inside…man-o-man, this place is jam-packed with all kinds of instruments. Enough to make about three full bands. Like marching bands, for example. My brother, his name is Harold but everyone calls him Harry, he was in a marching band in high school. He played this little xylophone thing—not one of those real big ones that are about five feet long, but the kind that you can carry around and tap with a little ball on a stick. He used to practice it all the time. It kinda drove me a bit crazy but he did get pretty good at it. He learned all the stuff he needed to do in the band. And he could even play a bunch of Beatles songs—that's how good he was.

Clifford starts talking to the guy who is running the place, telling him he needs a case for the guitar he bought a couple days ago, the one with the busted string. Clifford starts telling him every little detail about how he's gonna start doing a gig in Jackson Square. From what I know about body language—and

I know quite a lot—I don't think the guy is all that interested in the details, but he pretends like he is. Clifford has to tell the guy everything. I hear him say something about his *Bojangles* routine. I'm hoping he's not planning to give a demo right here in the store.

Meanwhile, I poke around hunting for an instrument. Something easy to play like I already said. I pick up a trombone. It's in pretty bad shape but I figure the notes are probably still okay. I try to blow into it but nothing comes out. Well maybe it lost some of the notes. I do the same thing with a trumpet, but it's even worse. All I get is a bunch of growling sounds. I think none of the instruments work all that well.

I don't see a tuba. Probably not a huge demand for tubas is my guess. And anyway, they're big as shit. The more I think about it, it's not something I feel like lugging through the French Quarter. Then, right there in front of me is the perfect instrument—a harmonica. In fact, a bunch of harmonicas. All different sizes. A little tiny thing about two inches long and a giant one about twelve inches long and every size in between.

I've seen people play harmonicas and it doesn't look all that tough to do. Like Bob Dylan, for example. He plays one that's attached to a harmonica holder around his neck and all he does is blow in and out. Yeow, get a load of that, I could play the thing with Clifford while he's strumming and singing and jumping.

I pick up a harmonica, one that's about six inches long, and take it over to where Clifford is talking to the man. It looks like he got what he was looking for. A sorta beat up old guitar case.

"Two dollars," the guy says.

Clifford's eyes light up.

"It's been around forever. Need to get rid of it," the guy says.

Clifford pulls out his wallet and pays.

"How about this?" I say to the guy, showing him the harmonica.

"That?"

I want to say, "No, you Bozo…do you see me holding a tuba?" But I don't. I just say, "Yeah…the harmonica."

One thing I learned from working at the hotel is to not get shitty with people…well, HR is who told us that because, let me tell you, there are some real buttheads who come to the hotel. Real buttheads! I mean all day long when you come right down to it. But I've got myself pretty well trained to deal with all those nitwits.

It's another reason why I'll be a good shrink. You've really got to be careful as hell about what you say. More so than any other kind of doctor. I mean, if a regular doctor says something shitty to you, you might think the guy's just in a bad mood, like maybe he's horny maybe and doesn't feel like working. I know all about that stuff because it's how I get sometimes when I'm hoping to run into Ramona, like when I haven't seen her in a while. But shrinks have to be real cool about stuff like that. Okay, I may have to work on it a bit yet. Even so, I already have a lot of patience when you consider how much time I spent the other day getting granny stretched out after the two-hour buggy ride.

When we leave the store, Clifford says, "Wanna hear something crazy?"

I wait to hear.

"They have this place down the street that has these real good beignets. I went there last time I was over here. Wanna get some?"

"Nah, not now. I need to get back," I tell him.

I show him the harmonica and blow a couple of notes in and out. It seems pretty easy. I can probably master it in a day or two.

14

When I get back, I mostly lay low for a while until it's time for work. I think about doing my Charlie Chaplin routine a little but I hold off and start blowing and sucking notes on the harmonica. Like I said, it's not as difficult as it might seem but then I probably have inherited a lot of skill with musical instruments when you consider how good my brother, Harry, is with his mini xylophone. I don't spend a lot of time with the harmonica because I can tell it's gonna pretty much be a snap. Tons easier than the tuba, that's for sure.

Work is pretty boring. No conventioneers or cowboys with saddlebags full of belt buckles or anything. I don't even see Eddie Clabberman with his horse and buggy. Might be it's his day off.

Sort of a lot of people all day long, but also plenty of time to go inside for iced tea. Wow, it's wicked hot! I think the three cowboys checked out. Musta sold all their buckles or got some store to peddle them.

At eight I go down to Napoleon's for a plate of red beans and rice like always. You can see I'm the kind of person who can get stuck in a routine. But I don't mind, especially if it's something I like doing. It's probably why I'll be a good shrink.

I'm real glad when my shift is finally over. I hang up my coat and stick my clip-on bowtie in the pocket and put my cap on the shelf.

On my way home, I stop in at The Chart Room. This much I can tell you though, I have no plans to get stuck yakking with that yo-yo Horace, not that he'd actually want to talk to me or any other Rat, for that matter.

Anyway, when I get to The Chart Room, Eddie Clabberman is there sucking on a Budweiser. He sets the mug down on the coaster that he rearranges in exactly the right place. He moves it just a little to the left and a little to the right and then back to the center again and then a little closer to himself—like a millimeter. Yikes! It's what shrinks call being anal-compulsive, from what I already know.

He tells me he had the day off, just like I suspected (part of that great radar stuff I have). He says he spent most of the day working on his tome. Says he made pretty good progress but that his characters are starting to get a little mixed up because he has so many of them. He told me how many but I don't remember what he said. A lot is all I remember.

Just then Sab and Joey come floating into the bar. They just got back from the Gulf Coast and you can tell everything must have been pretty good because they're both sorta tanned and happy looking. Sab thanks me for getting his mail, and then says they ran into Horace when they were coming down Conti Street on the way over from Joey's.

"He's got some kind of an incredible photo he wants me to see," Sab says. You can tell Sab's not buying a word of it. Who would? "He said he'd be here in a half hour or so."

The bartender sets down a *Corona* for Sab and a gin and tonic for Joey. Sab looks at his watch.

"If he comes by, tell him you haven't seen us," Sab says. 'We'll be over at Joey's...but don't tell him that."

Sab and Joey drink up and are out the door before Horace can corner them for the night.

I stay at The Chart Room for quite a while, mostly talking to Eddie. The place is nice and cool inside and it's pretty lively—quite a few Rats inside.

I leave and walk up along Bienville. It's dark and I can smell the spilled beer. I'm thinking about lots of stuff I got planned. Probably next year I'll get serious about doing whatever I need to do to become a shrink someday. Take some courses at Tulane or LSU maybe...the stuff I'll need to get into medical school. And yeah, I'll be a pretty damn good shrink considering all the junk I learned from working at the hotel. If nothing else, it's been good training for when I really need to deal with all kind of people.

I turn and head down Royal for a few blocks. When I get to Ramona's place, she's standing on the balcony looking down at the hot street below.

"Hey...Rubin," she calls. "Wanna come up?"

Oh Boy, do I ever!

www.ingramcontent.com/pod-product-compliance
Lightning Source LLC
LaVergne TN
LVHW091007080826
845145LV00003B/1163

* 9 7 8 1 7 3 6 8 1 0 1 0 1 *